The Philodendrist Heresy

The
Philodendrist Heresy

Book One of *The Heresy Series*

Jed Brody

Stormbird Press

Stormbird Press

Stormbird Press is an imprint
of Wild Migration Limited.

PO Box 73, Parndana, South Australia.
www.stormbirdpress.com

First published by Moon Willow Press, 2012.
Published by Stormbird Press, 2019 and 2021.

Cover design by Júlia Both.
Typeset by Stormbird Press with Antique Olive and Kazimir.
Forest illustration by Potapov Alexander/Shutterstock.

National Library of Australia and State Library of South Australia
Legal Deposit

Brody, Jed, 1974—Author

The Philodendrist Heresy

ISBN 13: 978-1-925856-11-8 (pbk)

ISBN 13: 978-1-925856-12-5 (ebk)

1. Science Fiction | 2. Action & Adventure | 3. Dystopian | 4. Nature

*The publishing industry still pulps millions of books every year when
new titles fail to meet inflated sales projections—ploys designed to
saturate the market, crowding out other books.*

*This unacceptable practice creates tragic levels of waste. Paper
degrading in landfill releases methane—a greenhouse gas emission
23 times more potent than carbon dioxide.*

*Stormbird Press prints our books 'on demand', and from sustainable
forestry sources, to conserve Earth's precious, finite resources.*

We believe every printed book should find a home.

dedicated to the archangels

Poems are made by fools like me, but only God can make a tree.

—Joyce Kilmer

Publisher's note

It's a breath-taking figure to contemplate. Nearly half of *Earth's* estimated 5.8 trillion trees cleared by humans. Grand old trees are falling fast.

Without trees, all hope seems lost, yet we continue to wipe these precious beings from the tropics for cattle, soybeans, and palm oil; from temperate regions by climate-driven wildfires; and from the planet's single largest biome—the boreal forests of Scandinavia to northern Canada through logging and ecosystem decline.

Most people understand we will struggle to survive in a world without trees, and yet, so many forests, that have stood for hundreds of years, now face extinction. These devastating losses should surely be mourned on a deep cultural level, enough to halt the terrible decline, and yet, we find ourselves in a space where brave, activist authors such as Jed Brody feel duty-bound to pen *The Heresy Series* as a siren call for the preservation and resurrection of the *Earth's* great forests.

Stormbird originally acquired Brody's dystopic series because his two brilliant books questioned, speculated and critiqued what our world would look like without trees. We embraced their underlying message and narrative brilliance, and imagined a future where humanity had failed to respond to deforestation in time.

We released Brody's *The Philodendrist Heresy* in 2019, and planned the release of the sequel, *The Entropy Heresy*, for early 2020. But then climate chaos wildfires razed our office, turned the surrounding fields to ash, and vaporised the ancient trees that had stretched their branches over us every day.

When people speak about wildfires, they often fail to grasp the scale of loss—not only to humans, but to the thousands of plants and animals, as well as coastal and river ecologies that once flourished downstream of fire zones.

Our entire ecosystem depended on trees, and it was in grave pain.

As the months crept along, we watched the blackened landscape struggle to survive without the living presence of its wise elders, now frail, charcoal skeletons. *The Heresy Series* came to have deeper, personal meaning to our team. Without huge eucalypts, graceful she-oaks, and charismatic banksia trees, our community became impoverished in ways we are only now beginning to understand. Forests affect people. When great trees burn or fall, we feel a life-changing wound to our soul.

Large, old trees are among the biggest organisms on *Earth*. They are keystone structures in forests, woodlands, savannas, and agricultural landscapes, playing unique ecological roles not provided by younger, smaller trees. Yet, populations of large, old trees are being annihilated throughout the world. This holds serious implications for ecosystem integrity and biodiversity—for humanity.

Let us hope, for all our sakes, that we heed Brody's warning, and that his work remains brilliant, compelling fiction, not prescience of times to come.

After all, even if we could live in a world without trees, who would want to?

Margi Prideaux
Publisher, Stormbird Press
November 30, 2021

1

Danielle Gasket paused at the shelf of scarves. She ran her fingers over the tall, rumpled heaps. The scarves were rough and crinkly, and they scratched audibly against her fingertips. She lifted a scarf that had blue and purple stripes. Humming softly, she returned it to the pile and selected one with gold and burgundy checkering. She wrapped it twice around her neck and tugged gently at the ends. One end was split, halfway across its width. Sighing and shaking her head, she removed the scarf and dropped it on the floor.

"Maintenance," she said.

A green maintenance drone trundled over, extended its hose, and with a loud slurp inhaled the defective merchandise.

Danielle dug through the piles of scarves in search of gold and burgundy checkering. Dozens of scarves spilled onto the floor and were promptly slurped up by the maintenance drone.

"Aha!" Danielle said with a smile, drawing another gold and burgundy scarf from the heap. But then she frowned. The far end of this scarf was also split halfway across its width. She tossed it on the floor and rummaged deeper into the mound of scarves.

"Maintenance," she said crossly. The drone scurried back from wherever it had gone.

Near the bottom of the heap, Danielle found another scarf with the desired pattern. She unwound it from the tangle and winced to see the same defect.

"Danielle Gasket! I thought I recognized your voice!" said a man who arrived and leaned against the shelf. He had long, black dreadlocks and a gray goatee. "You always had a temper!"

"Tommy Farad! I haven't seen you for months!" Danielle said, hurrying over to hug him gently. "How's your asthma?"

"A little better," he said with an almost imperceptible wheeze. "I've been breathing a lot of the orange vapor."

"Doesn't that sting your eyes and throat?" Danielle asked.

"It does," he said, "but at least I can draw a

satisfying breath some of the time." He inhaled slowly with a small rattle in his chest. "How's your stomach?"

"It still hurts after I eat, of course." Danielle said, "But usually not for the rest of the day. And I have diarrhea only once or twice a day now. I've been trying to eat almost entirely unseasoned food, except maybe salty 0.1. On a rare occasion, I add sweet 0.2."

"You really know how to treat yourself right!" Tommy said with a smile. "I remember what your mom told us during playgroup: Your arm muscle hurts when you lift weights. So of course your stomach is going to hurt when you digest food. To build strong arms, you have to lift weights, even though it hurts your arms. And to grow big and strong, you have to eat, even though it hurts your stomach!

"It's funny, I thought everyone grew up hearing that. But you know, I've done some traveling lately. When I tell people your mom's proverb, they slap their foreheads. 'Of course!' they say. 'Why hadn't we thought of that!'"   Danielle laughed. "It does make sense."

"How's your brother?" Tommy asked. "Still at the athletic academy in block D4A?"

"Yeah," Danielle said. "He's still training at hopscotch. He can complete the hundred-square in under twenty seconds."

Tommy whistled. "He's a speedy one, that Derek."

"He is. And yet, my dad says that the champions thirty years ago could do it in twelve or thirteen." Danielle lowered her voice. "Do you ever get the feeling that something's going wrong? Not just a little wrong, but terribly, terribly wrong?"

Tommy narrowed his eyes. "I'm sure I don't know what you're talking about, Danielle."

"Like this scarf," Danielle said. "Split at the end. This is the third scarf I found with this defect. How do you explain this? Is the factory breaking down? Where were the maintenance drones responsible for the factory?"

Tommy placed his hand on Danielle's arm. "It's just a scarf," he said.

"And what maintains the maintenance drones? Did you ever think about that? Why does nobody ever talk about that? What about the factories that make our food? Are they breaking down too? Is that why everyone's sick?"

Tommy squeezed Danielle's arm with sudden violence. "You have a great imagination, Danielle," he said mildly. "Have you ever considered studying the literary arts at the university? I think the university is a great place for people with wild imaginations, don't you? I'm sure that you can imagine," he leaned close, "worse places."

Danielle gasped at the pain in her arm. She rested her chin on Tommy's shoulder and pressed her lips against his ear.

"How did you get that scar under your eye?" she asked.

Tommy relaxed his grip and pulled away. "It's great seeing you, Danielle. I always liked you. Keep out of mischief, you hear? I can remember another good piece of advice that your mom gave us during playgroup: If there's something that no one's doing, that's because it shouldn't be done! If there's something that no one's asking about, that's because no one has the answers!"

Tommy looked around the warehouse. A young couple pushed a baby in a stroller; all three of these individuals had runny noses in need of wiping. An elderly couple inspected canes in a tall basket.

"How did you get that scar?" Danielle repeated in anger and in fear.

Tommy tightened his grip again. "Don't wake the baby. It's liable to throw a tantrum, and then everyone will be sorry."

Danielle glanced at the baby. She turned back to Tommy. "The baby isn't sleeping," she hissed.

Tommy leaned into Danielle's ear. "That's not the baby I'm talking about."

He kissed her cheek and took off, limping heavily.

A poster of a steel bowl was tacked to the door of the restaurant. Danielle entered and smelled the caustic odor of orange vapor. It was a breach of etiquette to request vapors outside of established areas or private residences, but everyone recognized that vapors were unavoidable; some asthmatics fainted after just a few minutes without any orange vapor. Danielle's eyes began to water, and she sighed. She heard the belches, moans, and occasional gagging noises of the diners.

She got in line for the food dispenser. An unusually rotund woman stood in front of her and ordered sweet 1.0, salty 0.5, sour 0.0, bitter 0.0, temperature 1.0. The woman walked toward a table with her bowl of piping hot, gray porridge. Danielle grabbed a steel bowl from the top of the pile and shook off the water droplets. She placed it under the dispenser and ordered, "Sweet 0.0, salty 0.1, sour 0.0, bitter 0.0, temperature 0.5." The dispenser plopped tepid, gray mush into her bowl. She took a spoon from the tray and found a seat at the window. Caustic orange fumes spiraled around her head. She coughed and wiped her eyes.

The first spoonful was always the worst. Chewier morsels were embedded deeper in the gelatinous slime. She gasped in displeasure as she swallowed. Immediate cramps sprang up in her abdomen, and a searing pain pierced the center of her stomach. She held her spoon in a tight fist and shoveled down her meal. She burped wetly and spat on the floor.

"Maintenance," she whimpered. Several minutes elapsed before a drone arrived to slurp up the spittle.

Pressing both hands against her stomach, Danielle stood up. She collapsed into a low stoop at the pain in her stomach, and she slowly forced herself erect. She walked over to the drink dispenser and ordered.

"Temperature 0.7."

Steaming water, just slightly grayish, sprayed into the steel cup. Danielle gulped it down, gagging at the oily film it left in her mouth. She belched three times and dropped the cup to be inhaled off the ground by a maintenance drone.

Staggering outside, she began walking in the minus y direction toward block F7A. Riding a taxi would be faster, but a little exercise usually mitigated her pains. She passed a conservatory, a theater, and a paint factory. She came to a stone fountain from which iridescent green water usually gushed, but now it was dry. No one was sitting on the benches near the fountain. Two empty leisure carriages rolled by, and then Danielle sat down and coughed.

"Blue vapor," she said.

Small holes opened in the gray street tile beneath her, and blue vapor jetted out. It slowed and dispersed as it rose, forming a cool mist at the level of her head. She breathed deeply, feeling a dull throb in the back of her throat. The blue vapor did nothing for her stomach pain, but it made her alert and energetic. Unfortunately, it also made her lips and fingers quiver.

A scrawny young man sat down next to her.

"You like blue vapor too? It's my favorite," he said, running his bony fingers through his thin hair. "We're odd, you know, you and I favoring the blue vapor. That's rare. Most folks our age like the white vapor. It dims the senses, makes the troubles go away. It's a kind of sleep, even when awake. You know something, there's an established blue-vapor restaurant in block F8B. Right above us. I'd sure like to show it to you some time."

"I just ate," Danielle said. "Food is the last thing I want."

"Then let's ride in a leisure carriage," the man said. "We can fill it with blue vapor, to match the paint on the carriage. It's as though the leisure carriages were designed for us who like the blue vapor."

"You're extremely unattractive," Danielle said.

"Well, well," he said. "Who said anything about attraction? Let's just ride a carriage as friends. Oh, and don't mind my feelings. It's well established that unattractive people don't have any."

"I'm sorry," Danielle said. "I'm just not feeling well. I shouldn't take it out on you. I'm sorry. My name's Danielle Gasket."

"I'm Jerry Reticle," he said. "And I don't know anyone who's feeling well. It's kind of funny that the word 'well' even exists."

"I suppose," Danielle considered, "it could be

useful in such sentences as, 'My boil is draining well.'"

"Or, 'This scarf mops up my gooey sneezes very well,'" he answered.

"Or, 'That tuba ensemble ought to disguise the sounds of my explosive diarrhea quite well,'" Danielle laughed.

"Or, 'These heavy curtains may muffle my dying screams all too well,'" Jerry said.

"Oh, thank you for that laugh," Danielle said through quivering lips. Her unsteady fingers adjusted her scarf. "I'm feeling a little better. Much better, in fact. Almost, I'm feeling—dare I say the word—well."

Jerry smiled. "Now, how about that leisure ride?"

"Okay," Danielle said. "Though I can't take any more blue vapor. Vapor off."

The pores in the street tile closed. Danielle gasped and quivered, not unpleasantly, for several moments.

"If you want something different," Jerry whispered, "I've got some yellow pills."

"What!" Danielle said. "Where did you get those? Don't you know they cause insanity? Haven't you been to a pill burning?"

"Of course," Jerry said. "That's where I got them. People were so busy shouting slogans and setting things on fire, they were hardly paying attention to anything. I reached toward the pile of pills, pretending to drop some in, but I grabbed a handful instead. Wish I'd grabbed more."

"What's it like when you take one?" Danielle asked.

"The bliss that surpasses understanding," Jerry said. "As though all the pleasure experienced by a hundred million people throughout their lives were rolled into a ball and compressed into every pore of your skin."

"Have you experienced any of the warning signs of impending insanity?" Danielle asked. "Nightmares? Angry voices calling your name when no one's around? Bright flashes on the backs of your eyelids?"

"No," Jerry said. "The risk of insanity doesn't bother me. What bothers me is the projectile vomiting that occurs every time a pill wears off. The serious addicts poke through the vomit in search of any remnants of the pill. But I don't believe the rumors that the pills cause insanity. I think that's a scare tactic. I think someone, somewhere, is hoarding the pills and doesn't want anyone else to want them."

"I don't know," Danielle said. "I've heard that the former addicts are the fiercest burners."

"If that's true, then the pills really do cause insanity," Jerry said. "Nothing's more insane than burning those things."

He coughed for some time and wiped his mouth. Danielle's stomach hurt.

"Leisure carriage," Jerry called.

Several pedestrians and a red medic vehicle passed by. Then a blue leisure carriage approached and slowed to a stop. With a comical flourish of his arm, Jerry indicated that Danielle was to board first. She stepped on and slid to the far end of the blue, padded seat. A seam separated the base of the seat from the back support. A safety belt slithered out of the seam and around her waist. The belt clicked into a buckle emerging near her hip. A second safety belt clicked shut around Jerry's gaunt body, and the carriage began to roll.

"What's the longest you've ever ridden on a leisure carriage?" Jerry asked.

"Probably six or seven hours," Danielle said.

"That's nothing," Jerry said. "I fell asleep on one and woke up nine hours later in an arithmetic library in precinct $x = 0.02$, $y = -0.03$, $z = 0.09$. I must've been dreaming about long division."

"I didn't know leisure carriages could function when you're asleep," Danielle said. "How does it know which direction increases your pleasure when you're not even aware of what's around you?"

"As far as I know," Jerry said, "it just scans the pleasure response of your brain, like normal. If the pleasure response increases, the carriage continues what it's doing. If the pleasure response decreases, the carriage tries something new. In normal operation, you're looking around, and your pleasure depends on the sights around you. When you're asleep, your pleasure is independent of what's around you, so the carriage responds only to what you're feeling in your dreams."

"Except that when you're sleeping, excessive noise is unpleasant, so the carriage is repelled by noise and attracted to silence. That's probably why you ended up in a library. Especially a library likely to be deserted at all hours of the day and night."

Jerry chuckled and scratched his throat. "Good thinking," he said. "You're probably right."

Their leisure carriage passed several apartments and a warehouse known for bonnets. It slowed near the warehouse door, where pedestrian traffic was heavy. The carriage circumvented an inexplicable heap of typewriters in the center of the road. Then it approached a door to the tunnel.

"Good," Danielle said. "We're getting out of F8A."

The tunnel door opened, and the carriage rolled inside. When the door shut behind them, their only source of illumination was the light in the front panel of the carriage. The blue light cast long, jittery shadows across Jerry's face as the carriage accelerated down the tunnel. The rumble of an unseen vehicle grew deafening and then receded. Danielle coughed at the astringent fumes, and the rush of air swept her hair behind her.

"Do you live in F8A?" Jerry asked.

"Yeah," Danielle said, "if you can call it living."

"You don't like your home?"

"I don't know any place that I really like," Danielle said. "Everywhere I look, things seem to be breaking down a little. It scares me, and no one even wants to talk about it. I don't really like anything I see. I think I'm happiest in the blackness of the tunnel. The darkness is soothing. It's exciting not to know where you're going, and not having to decide is relaxing. Although I have to wonder, how do the carriages even work in the tunnel? How do they know which way to go, and when to exit?"

"I think it's just like when you're dreaming," Jerry said. "If, for any reason, your pleasure response increases when the carriage is going fast, it will accelerate. If your pleasure response decreases, it will decelerate. When you get tired of the tunnel, deceleration will increase your pleasure because you know you need to decelerate to exit."

"That makes sense," Danielle said, "and I've often thought the same. But what I'm getting at is, what actually makes them work? How would I build one if I wanted to?"

"Why would you want to put yourself through such toil?" Jerry said. "Our forebears, in their wisdom and love, created the machines so that we might enjoy leisure..."

"...leisure they sacrificed on our behalf," Danielle recited. "Yes, we all learn this from our parents. Just as we learn that the machines were perfected so that there's no reason anyone should try to improve them or invent new ones. We learned to consider all they make for us: our food, our clothing, our air. As needed, they repair or replace our instruments of leisure. But do you really believe that improvement is impossible? Don't you think our food could be made to taste better, or least have a more consistent texture?"

Jerry looked away uncomfortably. "Our forebears, in the perfection of their wisdom, considered all the needs of their progeny," he said. "They looked far, infinitely far, into the future. No detail was left unattended. And then, in their humility and their mercy, they left no record of their strenuous mental exertions..."

"...so that we would not be baffled at their brilliance and shamed by our own cognitive limitations," Danielle finished. "Why are you repeating what every child hears? Don't you think for yourself?"

"I've seen bad things happen to people who think for themselves," Jerry said.

The hairs on Danielle's arms stood on end, and her pulse quickened. "This is the second time I've heard this today," she said. "What's going on? What do you know that I don't?"

Just then, a tunnel doorway opened, and the

leisure carriage exited the tunnel. The bluish gleam of the ceiling made Danielle blink. Several taxis passed, spewing gray exhaust, and Jerry coughed for some time. They were at the back of a crowd of spectators, many of whom had their fingers jammed in their ears. A marching ensemble of piccolo players paraded past the crowd. It was unclear whether the musicians were all attempting to play the same song, although they were all clearly attempting to play louder than the rest.

"That sounds the way broken glass tastes," Jerry shouted over the piercing din.

"And the way barbed-wire earmuffs feel," Danielle hollered.

The leisure carriage meandered away from the parade. To their right, a group of children played with jump ropes and hula-hoops, while a maintenance vehicle inhaled crumbled bricks on the left. The crowd thinned, and the carriage picked up its pace. Typical apartments, restaurants, and warehouses were dominant along this street.

"Do you know what precinct we're in?" Jerry asked.

"No," Danielle said, "but the carriage will take us home when that's what we want."

"Don't you just love how we don't need to be conscious of how to get home from here? The carriage must be able to scan some part of our brains that we aren't aware of."

"Even I have to admit that our forebears did an amazing job on the leisure carriages," Danielle said. "I just wish they'd shown the same attention to pleasure when they designed the food dispensers."

"Nobody likes to die, and nobody likes to eat," Jerry said. "Our forebears couldn't change those basic facts."

"I suppose you're right," Danielle sighed.

The road ahead was empty of vehicles. Colorful banners hanging from apartment windows spanned the street. Strewn along the ground were metal poles of various lengths and widths. The leisure carriage lurched and shuddered as it ran over the poles, sending the smaller ones spinning.

"This is kind of fun," Danielle said, as the lurching carriage tossed them back and forth.

"I think the poles are getting bigger," Jerry said. "I'm not sure we'll be able to make it over all of them."

"What's that up ahead?" Danielle asked. "Beyond the banners. Is that a shed on stilts?"

"I think so," Jerry said. A sudden lurch of the carriage sent his face rushing almost into his knees. "I've never seen anything like that before."

"Me neither," Danielle said.

With a loud crack, the carriage went still.

"What happened?" Jerry said. "We both want

to approach the shed on stilts. Why would the carriage think we want to stop?"

"I think it broke," Danielle said. "I think I saw something fly out of the front panel. You can see that something's missing here, underneath the light. We're missing some kind of rectangular cartridge."

"That's impossible," Jerry said. "Machines don't break. Our forebears, in their kindness and their love, in their brilliance and their glory, provided for the continual maintenance and renewal of the vehicles. Our tiny brains were mercifully spared the exhausting details."

"I'll show you," Danielle said. "I think the cartridge is somewhere on the ground beneath us. I saw it bounce off a pole and skid under the carriage."

She pressed the button on her safety-belt buckle, but nothing happened. She pressed again as hard as she could.

"The front panel's not all that's broken!" she exclaimed. "My safety belt doesn't even work."

"Don't worry," Jerry said. "I'll save the day! I'll check below for the cartridge."

He got out and looked under the carriage.

"I can't believe it! You're right! Something is down there, with one blue end that matches the carriage."

"Bring it up so I can see it," Danielle said, squirming in frustration against the belt.

"I'm afraid to stick my arm in front of the rear wheel," Jerry said. "What if the carriage spontaneously springs to life and runs over my arm?"

"Have you ever heard of anyone getting run over by any vehicle?"

"Of course not," Jerry said. "They were designed not to. But this one's obviously not working properly."

"Then you'll just have to be courageous," Danielle taunted. "We're having a remarkable adventure together, and you can either let it continue or cut it short by fetching me some scissors."

"No! Not the scissors!" Jerry said. "I don't want the adventure to end. Fine, I'll reach under the carriage. But you'd better call the medic if I faint in pain with cracked arm bones protruding through my skin."

"It's a deal," Danielle said.

She heard Jerry draw a raspy breath and cough.

"Got it!" he called. "Here it is!"

He sat next to Danielle and handed her the cartridge. Its surface was dented and metallic, and it felt light enough to be hollow. One end was painted blue.

"Now what?" Jerry asked.

"I guess I just pop it back in," Danielle said. "How hard could it be?"

She positioned the cartridge in front of the

cavity. She exerted gentle pressure against the cartridge, but it did not enter the cavity. The she gave the cartridge a spirited shove, and it screeched all the way in. The carriage jolted and began to roll. The poles on the ground slid and clattered in response.

"You fixed it!" Jerry said. "I've never seen anyone fix a machine before!"

"The adventure continues!" Danielle said.

"Mysterious shed on stilts, here we come!" Jerry said. "Although, it looks like we're turning around. That doesn't make any sense; we both want to see the shed up close."

"I don't know," Danielle said. "Maybe we lost interest in it."

The carriage rumbled over the poles on the road. Each clanging impact jarred both passengers.

"It sure is in a hurry to get away from the shed," Jerry said.

"All this bobbing up and down is making me sick to my stomach," Danielle said.

The carriage finally cleared the last pole and sped furiously down the road. It spun to the right and entered a dim alley. A towering pile of stained rags blocked their passage, but the carriage tore right through it. Stinking rags flew into Danielle's face and lap.

"Ugh! What's on these rags?" Danielle said.

"I don't know, but help me get them off of you!"

They hastened to throw the rags off the carriage. Some of the rags were moist and left pink, sticky residue on their hands.

"Those are the most disgusting things I've ever touched," Danielle said, "and I've often soiled myself with diarrhea. What is that vile pink stuff?"

"I don't know, but we're about to get some more of it!" Jerry screamed.

The carriage had wheeled around and was speeding toward the very center of the rag pile. Danielle and Jerry groaned in unison as damp, reeking rags flooded the carriage.

"What's wrong with this leisure carriage?" Jerry wailed, fiercely elbowing the rags away from him.

"I must've put the cartridge in upside down!" Danielle said. "The carriage is trying to maximize our displeasure!"

"It's doing a great job of it," Jerry said, gagging at the odor and trying to wipe pink residue off his lips.

"Help me clear the way to the front panel!" Danielle said.

They pounded and kicked at the filthy rags until the cartridge was visible.

"I can't pull it out!" Danielle said. "It's jammed in there!"

"We'll just have to jump out of the carriage," Jerry said.

"I'm stuck in here, remember?"

"I'll go get scissors and hurry back with them," Jerry said.

"There's no telling where I'll be by then!" Danielle said. "I've never seen a leisure carriage go so fast! Wait, did you just hear something?"

"I just heard it again," Jerry said. "Louder this time. And again! It's more irritating than that piccolo ensemble."

"That's why the carriage is taking us there," Danielle said.

"We need a plan. And I have an idea!" Jerry said. "You seem smart. You make the plan."

"It's hard to concentrate with that noise," Danielle said. "It's like a saw blade grinding against a metal bowl."

The carriage zoomed along narrow streets with no pedestrians. Leaky paint cans, crumbling bricks, and rusty bookcases lay neglected in tall mounds. The carriage bashed through the obstacles as Danielle and Jerry shielded their faces with their arms. All the while, the piercing noise shrieked louder.

"That noise!" Jerry screamed. "A saw blade grinding against a metal bowl in the center of my skull!"

He closed his eyes and pressed his palms against his ears. He twitched irritably and pulled away when Danielle tapped his shoulder. Then the tapping grew urgent, and he opened his eyes.

"What is that?" Danielle shouted over the noise.

Their leisure carriage was in line behind two rusted taxis. Ahead was a corrugated metal door.

When a vehicle approached the door, the door split in the center and swung inward. After the vehicle cleared the doorway, the two halves of the door slammed back together.

"The noise is coming from inside the building," Danielle said. "I don't really want to go in there alone, but I understand if you want to jump out. Now's probably a good time, and your last chance, as we're next in line."

"I used to read the troubadour poetry," Jerry said in a quavering voice. "I longed for danger and stupefying peril. And now that it's here, I just want the safety of my own apartment. But if you hold my hand, I may be able to ride with you to the finish."

Danielle placed her hand in his. The door swung open before them. Her heart raced, and she winced at the metallic screech, now louder than ever. Jerry panicked and tried to leap away before their carriage crossed the threshold, but Danielle retained her grip on his hand, even when he pounded her shoulder and begged to be let go.

The door slammed shut behind them.

2

"Speak up! I can't hear you!" Danielle screamed into Jerry's ear. The shriek of shredding steel blurred her vision and made her teeth ache.

"Let go of my hand! You're hurting me!" Jerry bellowed.

"Oh! Sorry," Danielle said. She flinched as something clattered against the roof of their leisure carriage. "What was that?"

Jerry leaned his head outside the carriage. He jerked back inside, and a heavy piece of metal clanged against the ground next to him.

"There are hundreds of buckets of scrap metal suspended from chains!" he yelled. "They're traveling every which way, vertically and horizontally. They're swaying as they move, and pieces of metal are flying everywhere."

Danielle strained against her safety belt and looked outside the carriage. The darkness was broken by dull red lights flickering above her. Some of the red light spilled onto the ground, dimmed, and went out. Danielle leaned into Jerry's ear.

"I think the red light is coming from swaying cauldrons of molten metal, which are also suspended from chains," she shouted. "Some of the molten metal is spilling out onto the ground."

"Just in case we're not impaled by crushing spears of scrap metal cascading from above, the incendiary splashes will give us something to die in agony from."

"That's not the worst of our problems! Look ahead!" Danielle said.

They squinted and leaned forward. Their leisure carriage was slowly following the two rusted taxis that had entered this place before them. Ahead of the taxis was a red medic vehicle missing a tire. Giant steel jaws closed on the medic vehicle and grinded it for several minutes, shredding it thoroughly. A conveyer belt under the jaws whisked the wreckage out of the way, and the next vehicle in line rolled dutifully into the jaws. Just one taxi remained between the jaws and the leisure carriage.

Danielle grabbed her safety belt with both

hands and pulled with all her might. "I'm still stuck!" she wailed. "I understand if you want to leave me to my fate and—"

Jerry was already out of the leisure carriage. He cupped his hands around his mouth and shouted, "I'm not leaving you! I'm looking for something to use to cut your belt!"

"Be careful!" Danielle yelled. "If you look at the ground, you can see relatively clear areas that are not directly under the buckets of scraps and molten metal."

Jerry nodded and leaped to a clearing at the edge of a mound of sharp, twisted metal fragments. He grabbed at a fragment and pulled his hand back, bleeding from his fingers. He reached more cautiously for a smoother fragment but was unable to lift it.

"Jerry! Hurry!" Danielle pleaded. "The taxi in front of me is about to enter the jaws."

Coughing and shaking, Jerry found a small, sharp sliver of metal and ran to Danielle. She took it and sawed frantically at her safety belt.

"The belt is starting to fray, but too slowly! I don't have enough time!" she cried. Tears streamed down her face. Up ahead, the taxi rolled into the grinding jaws, and the leisure carriage advanced into its place at the front of the line. Jerry leaned against the front of the leisure carriage but was unable to retard its progress. His shoulders heaved as he coughed from exertion, and he clutched his chest with one hand.

"I wish I had a pill that made me strong," Jerry yelled.

"Jerry!" Danielle shrieked. "That gives me an idea! Give me a yellow pill!"

Jerry frowned.

"Not now!" he said. "You need to think! I understand that you want to die blissfully if you have to die, but I think you're smart enough to save yourself, if you concentrate!"

"That's what I'm doing!" Danielle hollered. "The upside-down cartridge is causing this carriage to maximize my distress and minimize my pleasure. When my brain registers pleasure, the carriage has to stop what it's doing and try something new. And nothing creates more pleasure than a yellow pill!"

Jerry's trembling hand shot into his pocket. He sprang out of the way of a falling cogwheel and handed Danielle a small pouch. She tore it open, and yellow pills spilled everywhere, just as the front bumper of the leisure carriage entered the steel jaws. Jerry wailed, either at Danielle's peril or at the loss of the pills. Danielle tossed a pill down her throat.

"Oh wow," Danielle giggled. "Oh wow."

The screech of shredding steel faded to a soft and soothing hum. Danielle hummed along.

"La la la, la la la," she tried to sing, but instead of sounds, iridescent bubbles floated out of her mouth. The bubbles swelled and spun, rising to a great height, and then burst into cascades of rainbow stars. The coolest, most refreshing fountain of drool bathed her lips and chin. Danielle had never been so happy.

And then, into her wonderland of happiness came the most irritating intruder. It was a voice, the most annoying voice she had ever heard. Nasal. Raspy. Wheedling. She didn't even know what "wheedling" meant; she just knew it was the best word to describe this voice. Nothing could possibly have been more annoying than this voice, except for the things it was saying.

"It's wearing off already, and then you'll be right back to where you started!" it said. "I know that thinking is the last thing you want to do right now, but I'm not smart enough to save you! You need to come up with a plan before the pill wears off entirely!"

The leisure carriage backed up steadily, clattering over steel shards and black lumps of solidified metal. Jerry jogged along beside.

"I already have a plan," Danielle cooed. "It calls for my hands. Have you seen them? They're feeling very...distant."

"Yes, they're at the ends of your arms, where they usually are," Jerry said impatiently.

"Oh, Jerry," Danielle sighed. "What help are you? I haven't seen my arms for weeks."

The leisure carriage wheeled about indecisively.

"We don't have time for this!" Jerry said. "Just tell me your plan."

"Oh, Jerry," Danielle sighed again. "I wish you'd go away. You're really bothering me. Your skeleton is shining so brightly, it's hurting my eyes. Also, you're really stupid. The carriage is trying to maximize my distress. So I need to register increasing distress as I increase my chances of breaking out of here. Now, where's that really sharp sliver of steel you brought me earlier?"

"For some reason, you're balancing it on top of your head," Jerry said nervously.

"Ah! Perfect!" Danielle said. "Now watch my genius spring into action."

She belched and broke wind.

"I don't feel so good," she said. She shook her head and blinked forcefully. "I suppose that's for the best."

She took the steel sliver off the top of her head. She pressed the point against the back of her left hand as she faced the corrugated door. The carriage lurched into action.

"What are you doing?" Jerry screamed.

"I'm not going fast enough to break the door," Danielle hissed. She drove the sliver deeper into her hand and wailed in pain. The carriage accelerated toward the door. Danielle tore through her skin from her knuckle to her wrist. She shuddered and vomited, lifted the steel sliver, and slashed again through the back of her hand.

The leisure carriage roared forward at top speed. Fearful for Danielle's safety, Jerry screamed and flailed his arms helplessly. Danielle squeezed shut her eyes, and the leisure carriage crashed against the door. Danielle was flung forward but halted by the safety belt, which drove deep into her abdomen. The carriage moved no further. Danielle rested her arms against her knees and moaned.

"That's the most incredible thing I've ever seen!" Jerry shouted into Danielle's ear. "I think the carriage is wrecked. You're safe! Just watch out for falling cogwheels and spear-like shards. And red-hot liquid metal. Especially that."

"You don't have to shout anymore," Danielle gasped. "Listen."

The metal jaws had gone silent. Buckets of scraps and cauldrons of molten steel swung from creaky chains. A loud, cascading clatter rang in the darkness.

"That's just scraps falling from a bucket," Danielle said. "I think." She wiped tears from her eyes and vomit from her lips. "How do I look?" she asked with a crooked smile.

"I've never seen anyone more beautiful," Jerry said. "How's your hand?"

"I think there's still a hand here under all this blood," Danielle said.

"A medic will take care of that as soon as we get out of here," Jerry said. "It looks like you battered a large enough hole in the door for us to squeeze through. And I found a better scrap of metal for sawing through your safety belt. This one has a kind of serrated edge."

Jerry began sawing at the belt. Danielle leaned her head against his shoulder.

"I'm sorry my shoulder's so bony," Jerry said.

"I'm sorry my face is so vomity," Danielle answered.

"I wouldn't want it any other way," Jerry said.

Danielle chuckled and closed her eyes.

"There," Jerry said. "You're free."

Danielle took a wobbly step out of the smashed leisure carriage. She slid on the blood that had flowed from her hand onto her shoes. She leaned against Jerry and made her way to the jagged hole in the steel door.

"I'm almost sorry this adventure is about to end," Jerry said.

"We're not out of here yet," Danielle said. "Who knows what zany hijinks could ensue?"

"I've had enough zany hijinks for today," Jerry said. "I'd like only tranquil hijinks from now on. Careful stepping through the hole in the door; it's really sharp."

Danielle stepped one leg over the bottom of the hole and ducked through it. She blinked against the light from the ceiling on the other side.

"Red 0.0, yellow 0.0, blue 0.1," she said. "Also: medic." The ceiling light dimmed to a dull blue.

Jerry clambered through the hole in the door. He coughed mightily and sneezed. He smiled weakly, limped over to Danielle, and collapsed.

"Jerry! What's wrong?" Danielle said.

"Some of the molten metal got on my foot," he said, wincing. "In all the excitement, I didn't notice the pain. Now, I notice it something fierce."

"I just called a medic," Danielle said. "You'll be okay." She put her good hand on his shoulder.

"You too," he said with a smile. His eyelids fluttered.

"Jerry! Stay with me," Danielle said. "Think of the excitement we just had! What was that place? Some kind of vehicle recycling factory?"

"You're so smart, Danielle," Jerry said, shaking his head sadly. "I've known only one other person as smart as you. It was my Uncle Gabe. Don't go the way he went, okay? Stay away from those literary arts. Leave the troubadour ballads where they belong, in the trash heap of antiquity."

"Jerry, you're not making any sense!" Danielle said. "How badly are you hurt?" Then she inhaled sharply. "The literary arts? Is that what you said? That's the second time today I heard a cryptic warning about the literary arts."

"It's really too bad, Danielle," Jerry said. His eyes filled with tears. "I could teach you so much. My uncle taught me so much. But he made too much noise. It woke the baby."

Danielle's grip tightened on Jerry's shoulder.

"Jerry! Speak clearly! No more riddles! Who is this baby?"

"It's the funniest thing, Danielle," Jerry said, tears dribbling past his hollow cheeks. He coughed and shook his head. "When the molten steel hit me, I was standing in a clear area. It didn't spill from a cauldron. I saw someone aim it at me. Ah! My foot!" He bent his leg and clutched his foot, moaning and rocking.

Danielle's pulse quickened, and she clenched her teeth. A red medic vehicle trundled over.

"Him first!" Danielle said, pointing at Jerry.

The vehicle extended its red hose and scanned Jerry's body. The hose settled by his ankle. A syringe extended from the hose and punctured his skin.

"No!" Jerry screamed. His eyes widened, and he shook once. The skin around the injection site blackened and sizzled.

"What happened?" Danielle cried. "I've never heard of medics harming people! I was trying to help you!"

"I have one more secret to share, Danielle," Jerry whimpered. Black fluid began to ooze from his nose and mouth. "Come closer," he gurgled.

Danielle pressed her face against his, wetting his eyebrows with her tears.

"My secret is this," he groaned, beginning to stiffen. "I set the whole thing up. I loosened the cartridge so it would fall out, and I tampered with your safety belt. This taught you that machines are dangerously fallible. I placed you in terrible danger, yet you outwitted the malfunctioning machine. This taught you confidence and self-reliance. I mentioned that I had yellow pills, which you needed to escape. This taught you that every challenge you face has a solution within your grasp. I'm dying, struck by an unseen enemy, leaving you alone in stupefying peril. This teaches you valor in the face of overwhelming odds. I gave my life to teach you this. Don't let me down."

He went silent. The red hose of the medic vehicle swayed toward Danielle.

"Cancel medic request!" she yelled.

The vehicle withdrew. Danielle removed the scarf from her neck and wrapped it around her bloody hand. She wiped her lips, took a final glance at Jerry, and ran as fast as she could in the other direction.

3

Danielle leaned against a dusty pinball machine in the middle of the road. She gasped for breath. Familiar, sharp pains flickered in her abdomen. Her legs quivered, and her wounded hand throbbed. Blood had soaked through the scarf and spattered on her clothes.

"Blue vapor," she said.

Blue tendrils wafted around the pinball machine. Danielle breathed deeply, and her lips began to shake as a wave of energy surged over her body. She needed to think clearly. The medic that had killed Jerry could easily have killed her as well. It could have ignored her verbal commands. It could have chased her. Even if she had been able to outrun it, other vehicles could have arrived to poison her or simply run her over. Whoever killed Jerry had allowed Danielle to live.

What would happen if she called a medic to repair her hand? She did not think it would kill her; if someone controlling the machines wanted her dead, she would be dead already. Still, she wanted to find a way to take care of herself. Machines were clearly untrustworthy, and the more she learned to make do without them, the better.

"Blue vapor off," Danielle said. The shaking in her fingers, caused by the vapor, was beginning to irritate her wound.

"Taxi!" she said. She dusted off the pinball machine while she waited. The ball was missing, though she couldn't find any hole that it could have fallen through. The taxi arrived, and she climbed inside.

"Block F8A in $x = 0.07$, $y = -0.11$, $z = -0.20$," she said. "The warehouse."

The taxi navigated a small labyrinth of overturned easels, and it entered the tunnel. Danielle closed her eyes in the darkness. She heard other vehicles passing. There were so many opportunities for fatal collisions. She had no ability to steer the taxi or slow it down. She lived at the discretion of the machines. This thought was somehow soothing. Since she had no control over whether she lived or died, she might as well relax.

She frowned. Maybe she did have some control over whether she lived or died. If she displeased whoever ruled the machines, she could expect an unhappy fate. Jerry's fate was unhappy, and apparently so was his uncle's. Jerry had said that she was as smart as his uncle, but she would prove that she was smarter. She would learn how to escape an unhappy fate, and she would not leave it to chance. She would seek out the forbidden knowledge, and she would somehow use it to her advantage.

The taxi emerged from the tunnel into a crowded street. Parents pushed strollers, young couples held hands, and children bounced large balls. The taxi meticulously avoided them all and made its way to the warehouse.

Danielle strode into the warehouse. The sharp scent of new fabric stung her throat and made her eyes water. She walked past rows of tablecloths, smocks, and socks. Her shoulder accidentally overturned a basket of boxing gloves.

"Maintenance," she said irritably.

She absently grabbed some new clothes from drab racks. She passed several children who were testing ping-pong paddles on one another's faces. In the back corner of the warehouse, she came to the scarf shelf. Her heart skipped a beat. There was only one scarf on the shelf, and it had exactly the same pattern as the one wrapped around her hand: gold and burgundy checkering. She lifted it and found the familiar defect, the split at one end. Under the scarf, she saw crude lettering in chalk: "We are watching you."

Her eyes darted around the warehouse. She saw no one, just long rows of shelves and racks. Unnerved, she crawled under the shelf and changed out of her bloodied clothing. A maintenance drone wheeled by and slurped up the discarded items. The drone departed with a loud creak and a puff of black exhaust.

Danielle unwrapped the blood-soaked scarf and examined her wounded hand. The two gashes met at her knuckle and her wrist, forming a kind of eye shape. She wrapped the new scarf around her hand. Her abdomen contracted painfully, and she grimaced.

She hastened out onto the street and passed a playground. A row of bathrooms made up the bottom floor of an adjacent building. She dashed to the nearest door, but it was locked. Grimacing, she staggered to the next bathroom, which was mercifully unoccupied.

Sighing with relief, she left the bathroom. She strolled idly for some time. Three old men sat on a park bench in a cloud of white vapor. Danielle held her breath as she passed. She did not crave numbness and forgetfulness at this time. Two medic vehicles hurried by in opposite directions, and an empty taxi wandered. Danielle called the taxi and climbed in.

"The nearest university," she said.

The taxi traveled for several minutes. It halted in a typical block with many restaurants, warehouses, apartments, and parks. The ceiling gleamed with a bright red light, probably red 1.0, yellow 0.0, blue 0.0. Banners hanging over the street read, "Photograph development in progress! Please do not alter lighting!"

The unusual lighting began to give Danielle a headache. When she stepped out of the taxi, the sour scent of photography chemicals made her gag. She followed signs to the university. Many young people sat on benches and loudly debated inconsequential matters. She found a map on the wall that identified the university's four main hallways: photography, arithmetic, literary arts, and oratory. She quickened her pace and proceeded to the department of literary arts.

The hallway was lined with rooms full of desks and bookshelves. Danielle could not imagine how anyone could read under this eerie red lighting. The priority on this block seemed to be the photography department.

Danielle did not know where to begin her research into the forbidden secrets. Jerry had said something about the troubadour ballads of antiquity, but Danielle did not know how the books were organized. Observing that some of the books lay in heaps on the floor, Danielle suspected that the books were not organized at all.

In some of the rooms, scholars sat at desks, furrowing their brows impressively as they read. In other rooms, scholars paced and read loudly from scrolls. Danielle wandered for some time, and then, with trepidation, approached a white-haired scholar who sat with his back to the door.

"Excuse me," Danielle said from the doorway. "You appear to be an eminent scholar, and I was hoping I could ask you some questions."

"I am sitting with my back to the door because I do not wish to be disturbed," the scholar answered. He spun his head around, causing his glasses to fly off his nose onto the floor.

"Oh dear," he said.

"Here, I got them," Danielle said.

"Thank you very much," the scholar said, sliding his glasses up his nose. "Very kind. Thank you. Now, where was I? Oh, yes. Please go away."

"Please," Danielle said. "I won't take too much of your time."

"You already have!" the scholar barked. "Skip the preamble! Ask your questions!"

"Thank you," Danielle said. "Can you tell me anything about the troubadour ballads of antiquity?"

The scholar scowled and tugged his long eyebrows. "Why would anybody be interested in those? The diction is archaic, the style is somehow both simplistic and ostentatious, and the symbolism is indecipherable, unless you're a specialist in archeolinguistics."

"I—I'm not sure," Danielle said. "A friend recommended the ballads to me. I just wanted to follow the suggestion."

"Some taste your friend has!" the scholar said. "Is this the same friend who picked out that shirt for you?"

"Yes," said Danielle. "It's also the same friend who taught you manners."

"Bravo!" the scholar chuckled. "I've always held that an acerbic wit is the mark of a first-class intellect. Because I like you, I'll be direct. There are no specialists in archeolinguistics outside of the central university in $x = 0.00, y = 0.00, z = 0.00$. The department of literary arts is in block B9F. Bring a coat. The entire block is an ice skating rink, so the temperature is 0.0."

Smiling, he turned back to his book.

"Thank you so much," Danielle said. "I, uh, actually have one more question."

The scholar stomped his foot.

"When I said I liked you, I didn't mean to invite you to stand here all day," he said.

"Thank you very much," Danielle said, taking a seat next to him. "My feet were getting tired."

The scholar held his head in his hands.

"Just ask your question," he moaned.

"Are there any scholars who study the way that the body recovers from injuries?" Danielle asked. "And don't tell me that this is what medic vehicles are for. The medics clean and dress the wounds, but after that, the body heals on its own. More generally, are there any scholars who study the way the body works when it's healthy?"

The scholar raised himself up in his seat.

"Do you know what I am?" he said.

"Um, a scholar?" Danielle said.

"A scholar, what?" he hollered.

"A scholar, sir?" Danielle said.

"No! I mean, I scholar of what. I sometimes omit prepositions when I'm angry," he said.

"How odd," Danielle said. "Anyway, you're a scholar of the literary arts?"

"Yes!" he said. "And was I born a scholar of the literary arts?"

"No."

"And was I born a master of the anapestic quatrains of precinct $x = -0.21$, $y = 0.02$, $z = 0.06$?"

"No," Danielle said.

"That's right!" the scholar said. "I am a scholar of things I didn't know when I was born. That's what makes it scholarship. I had to work. I had to read. I had to study. But! Was I born knowing how to blink?"

"Yes."

"Was I born knowing how to drool?"

"Yes," Danielle said.

"Was I born knowing how to wail at the top of my lungs?"

"I'm sure you were," Danielle said.

"That's why there can be no scholarship of the body. We're born knowing how to use it. That's why no respectable university has a department of urination studies. That's why there's no department of flatulence studies. So why don't you take your perspiration studies, and move along!"

"Don't you think," Danielle hissed, "it's worthy of study that the athletes of our time lag far behind the records of earlier champions? Don't you think it's worthy of study that people seem to be aging faster than before? My own mother says I look the way she did when she was ten years older than I am now."

"Nonsense!" the scholar said. "You look very sprightly for a woman in her thirties."

"I'm 22," Danielle said.

"That explains your want of maturity," the scholar said. "Come back when you're grown and ready to discuss some real scholarship."

Danielle glowered and stomped out of the room. Her belly ached, and her face was hot with anger. A young man jumped out of her way as she went through the door.

"He's such a brilliant man," the young man whispered. "Truly a first-class intellect. I hope to be like him some day."

"You've got a long way to go," Danielle grumbled. "You're showing no sign of an acerbic wit."

"Teach me!" he pleaded, trotting after her down the hallway.

She ignored him and exited the university. She walked through crowded streets, all illuminated by red light and reeking of photography chemicals. She found a warehouse and went inside to look for a coat. She picked a lightweight jacket with deep pockets. As soon as she left the warehouse, she called a taxi.

"Block B9F in precinct x = 0.00, y = 0.00, z = 0.00," she said.

Her abdominal pains intensified, but not to an unusual degree. The taxi took her into the tunnel, and the red light vanished behind her.

4

As soon as the taxi emerged from the tunnel, Danielle gasped at the cold. She could see her breath. She stepped out of the taxi and slid on the thin layer of ice that seemed to coat the entire street. Numerous people wearing ice skates skittered merrily by. Taxis and leisure carriages skidded slowly among the skaters, and several medic vehicles were positioned along the walls, presumably in anticipation of skating accidents.

Danielle shoved her hands in her pockets and looked around in wonder. Stone sculptures loomed tall throughout the street. Small choirs and orchestras competed for audiences. Colorful paintings decorated the outer walls of all the buildings. Some of the paintings featured geometric patterns, some featured imaginary scenes, and some featured frighteningly large eyes.

She glanced around in search of a directory. None was in sight, so she drove her heel against the ice and glided on one foot. With a little practice, she was able to move efficiently, and she fell down only once every few minutes.

She narrowly avoided a violin soloist, and she came to a small crowd facing an empty podium. She took her hands out of her pockets and shook her arms to warm them. A young man with a braided beard turned toward her. There were bells at the ends of the braids. They jingled.

"I like how you wear a scarf around your hand," he said. "Once I wore my pants on my head for about a week."

"Why did you do that?" Danielle asked.

"I don't remember," he said.

"Did white vapor have anything to do with it?"

"I don't remember," he repeated.

"I wouldn't expect that you would," Danielle said.

"Someone's about to recite the Doggerel of Janet Peptide," he said. "It's so beautiful, man. You should stick around for it."

"Actually," Danielle said, "I was hoping I might inquire—"

"I'm a tattoo artist," he interrupted. "I specialize in the buttocks."

"Tattoos ornamenting the buttocks, or tattoos depicting the buttocks?" Danielle asked.

"Both," he said, without a hint of a smile. "Perhaps you'd be interested?"

"Actually," Danielle said, "I'm a little squeamish around—"

"Quiet!" the man said. "The poem is about to begin!"

A short, bony woman clambered onto a stool behind the podium.

"The Doggerel of Janet Peptide," she began. "Favoring neither wisdom nor foolishness, I found wisdom. Favoring neither peace nor horror, I found peace. Favoring neither love nor hatred, I found love. Favoring neither joy nor sorrow, I found joy. Favoring neither self nor other, I found both. Favoring neither feast nor famine, I found enough. Favoring neither success nor failure, I found my destiny. Favoring neither body nor disembodiment, I found immortality."

The crowd responded with spotty applause. The man next to Danielle shook his head in awe. His bells jingled.

"That's so beautiful, man," he said. "So beautiful."

"Is the woman up there Janet Peptide?" Danielle asked. She pressed her hands in her pockets, beginning to shiver from the cold.

The man pulled his head back. His bells plinked against his chest.

"No, man," he said. "Janet Peptide was a troubadour of antiquity."

"That's unbelievable!" Danielle exclaimed. "That's exactly what I've come here to study! I'm especially interested in archeolinguistics. Do you know where I can found a scholar of this discipline?"

"We're standing right in front of the library of troubadour ballads. I think there's a hall dedicated to archeolinguistics. There's a directory next to the main door."

"I can't get over this coincidence," Daniele said. "I was just wandering the street at random, and I ended up in front of the very building I sought."

"There's no such thing as coincidence, man. You've just found your destiny, as Janet Peptide said."

"Well, thank you for your help," Danielle said.

She approached the directory and read the list of all the specialties related to the troubadour ballads of antiquity. Archeolinguistics was housed in the seventh hall to the right. Danielle entered the library. The floor inside was coated in ice, just like the floor outside. She rubbed her cold arms, and then she glided to the right. She tripped over a book and landed on her face.

She groaned and rubbed a painful bruise on her cheek. She rose unsteadily to her feet and proceeded with greater caution. She came to the seventh hall and entered it. Doors into small rooms lined both sides of the hall. The first door was closed and locked. The next two doors led to rooms cluttered with books and excess chairs. In the next room, a woman sat at a desk facing the hall. Tight, gray coils of hair bristled from her head. She wore bifocals and raised her eyebrows imperiously when she saw Danielle.

"Excuse me," Danielle said. "I'm hoping to speak with a scholar of archeolinguistics. Is that, perhaps, what you are?"

"Do you have an appointment with me?" the woman asked.

"Oh! Well, no, I'm afraid I don't," Danielle said.

"I knew that!" the woman said. "Do you know how I knew that?"

"No, I'm sure I don't," Danielle said.

"Because I never grant appointments to anyone! And do you know why that is?"

"No," said Danielle.

"Because anyone I teach ends up vanishing or dying a terrible death!"

"Why?" Danielle asked.

"I've told you too much already," the woman said. "I've already endangered your life. For your own sake, you'd better be going. Watch your back. Don't use medics unless you absolutely need to. Learn to take care of yourself. For example, take that bruise on your cheek. Just lay your face against the ice on the ground. That'll make it feel better."

"But I don't understand," Danielle said. "If your knowledge is so dangerous to people, why are you still alive?"

"It takes a lot of finesse to sow terror and blind panic among the masses," the woman said. "If one or two people are allowed to live and spread their tales of horror and woe, the message is disseminated far more effectively than if I were simply killed."

"So you've become a willing servant of whoever is terrorizing us," Danielle said.

"No, I wouldn't put it that way," the woman said. "I'm just trying to spare you, that's all."

"I accept full responsibility for whatever gruesome, grisly fate awaits me," Danielle said. "I just want to know what makes archeolinguistics such a lethal pursuit."

"Well, all right," the woman sighed, "but don't say I didn't warn you. Have a seat."

Danielle looked around. "You're sitting in the only chair in the room."

"Oh. Sorry," the woman said.

"Don't worry about it. There are plenty of chairs in the next room. I'll be right back."

"Shut the door when you return," the woman said.

"Okay."

Danielle returned with a chair and sat down. She breathed heavily and watched the chill of her breath waft out of her mouth.

"My name is Arlene Cilia," the woman began. "I am, to the best of my knowledge, the only surviving scholar of archeolinguistics. I attribute my survival to no personal merit or valor but to the whim of the warden, whom I will discuss in a moment. First, I need to ascertain your mastery of basic facts. Tell me, how many blocks are in a precinct?"

"A thousand," Danielle said.

"And how are they arranged?"

"In a cube, ten by ten by ten."

"And how are they named?"

"The location in the x direction is specified by the letters A through J. The location in the y direction is specified by the numbers 0 through 9. And the location in the z direction, like the x direction, is specified by the letters A through J. So, for example, the block in the most minus x, minus y, minus z corner of a precinct is named A0A."

"Fine," Arlene said. "And how many precincts are there?"

"201 times 201 times 201," Danielle said. "I can't do the arithmetic in my head."

"I don't know anyone who can," Arlene said. "The answer is 8,120,601. How are these precincts arranged?"

"The precincts are also arranged in a cube, 201 by 201 by 201."

"And how are they named?"

"Each of the three coordinates can take any value with two decimal places from -1.00 to +1.00. So, for example, the precinct in the far minus x, minus y, minus z corner is $x = -1.00$, $y = -1.00$, $z = -1.00$."

"Very well," Arlene said. "What is the total number of blocks?"

"Since there are 1000 blocks in a precinct, the total number of blocks is 8,120,601,000."

"Very good," Arlene said. "You remembered the total number of precincts. Your memory may prove to be a very useful asset. Now, tell me, what is to the minus x direction of the blocks beginning with A in the $x = -1.00$ precincts?"

"It doesn't matter," Danielle said, "because we have no way to find out. Even our forebears, in the fullness of their genius, did not have the answer to this question. Yet they had the wisdom, which we would do well to emulate, to not waste precious cognitive resources on an unanswerable question."

Arlene laughed. "And do you believe that?"

"Of course not," Danielle said. "I was just reciting what every child is taught."

"And so you were also taught that our forebears, in their wisdom and love, created the machines. Our forebears created the machines so that we might enjoy leisure, leisure that they sacrificed on our behalf. In the perfection of their wisdom, our forebears considered all the needs of their progeny. They looked far, infinitely far, into the future. No detail was left unattended. And then, in their humility and their mercy, they left no record of their strenuous mental exertions so that we would not be baffled at their brilliance and shamed by our own cognitive limitations. You've heard this all before?"

"Yes, of course," Danielle said.

"What you've just heard me recite is what I call the great lie," Arlene said. "Since it's a lie, something else must be the truth. I believe that the truth was known to the troubadours of antiquity. But, for fear of persecution, they did not proclaim the truth openly. Instead, they encrypted their secrets in elaborate symbolism. Every word in their ballads carries far more than its literal meaning. The secret, hidden meaning of each word is what we study in archeolinguistics.

"After centuries of research and debate, the scholars of archeolinguistics arrived at this conclusion: the troubadours of antiquity were preserving a creation myth that was ancient even in their own time. Now, you'll never find a troubadour ballad that explicitly addresses the creation myth. The ballads might describe the grief of a wrestling champion who is growing too old to defend his title, or the happy dilemma of a woman courted by nineteen suitors. But, for those who have mastered the secret symbolism, an entirely different story unfolds.

"It would take years to describe the symbolism. Each troubadour used a different set of symbols, and yet each ballad alludes to other ballads, so you have to be a true expert to weave together the hidden meaning. I'll just skip the centuries of scholarship and take you right to its result. Okay?"

Danielle nodded. Her hands quivered from either cold or excitement. Wrapped in the scarf, the gashes in her hand ached.

"According to this myth," Arlene continued, "our distant ancestors lived in a kind of a perfect setting called heaven. This heaven is thought to be far above us, far above $z = 1.00$. The air smelled good all the time, and the water tasted good all the time. The food tasted good, and swallowing it brought great satisfaction and pleasure to the stomach."

"That's not possible!" Danielle exclaimed, thinking of the aches in her abdomen that never totally went away.

"Strange as it sounds, this is the message the troubadours have for us," Arlene said. "And that's just the beginning. Our ancestors, in heaven, had a much higher ceiling over their heads than we do. They had no way to touch their ceiling, no matter how high they stacked things to climb on. Their ceiling changed color, but not on command, and not uniformly. It was as though a brilliant artist, far greater than any we have known, was forever creating new patterns to astound and delight. These were the patterns that our ancestors witnessed on their ceiling.

"When it was time for them to sleep, their ceiling went dark, almost to red = 0.0, yellow = 0.0, blue = 0.0, but gradually, so they had time to adjust. In the darkness, they were able to sleep deeply. But the ceiling was not entirely dark, for there were tiny pinpoints of light in dazzling patterns that slowly pirouetted above.

"When it was time to awake, a great fire rose up upon the ceiling, like the light of a billion candles. Though it was far too distant to touch, its soothing warmth could be felt on the skin. The great fire traveled from one end of the ceiling to the other, and then it vanished, just when it was time to sleep again. The majestic, timeless fire moved in a rhythm perfectly suited to daily human cycles.

"In heaven, our ancestors enjoyed the companionship of other living...things. They are difficult to describe. They were not humans, but they resembled humans more than they resemble our machines. They existed in great variety. Some had hair all over their bodies and their faces."

"That sounds like my brother," Danielle said. "I always suspected that he wasn't quite human."

Arlene smiled. "I assure you, you cannot imagine the beauty, grace, and diversity of these companionable...things. I think these things were known as angels, though there has been some debate over this point. Now, there were angels that lived in the waters, and angels that lived on the ground, and angels that somehow lived in the air. And all across the ground of heaven, there dwelled many millions, nay, billions of archangels.

"The archangels lived for hundreds or thousands of years, and they grew to be hundreds of feet tall. They inspired awe and reverence in all who beheld them. In appearance, they resembled mighty pillars with craggy surfaces, many twists and turns, and dozens of towering arms. Many angels, miniature in comparison, lived cradled in the sturdy arms of the archangels.

"And there, in the peace and perfection of heaven, amid sonorous choirs of angels and serene congregations of archangels, with hearts full of wonder and delight, lived our own ancestors! They sat at the feet of the archangels and touched them with their hands. And thus they lived in harmony for a million years.

"Sometimes an arm fell crashing off an archangel, and the humans would accept the gift with gratitude and humility. They would use the arm of the archangel to make fire or to build simple tools. Then, in their pride and their arrogance, they decided that heaven needed some improvements. Some remodeling. So from the flesh of archangels, fallen from old age, they fashioned themselves small huts to live in.

"Before long, the crafty, cunning humans were impatient for the archangels to fall. So the humans began to slaughter the archangels. At first, the slaughter was limited to isolated pockets; far from the centers of human activity, the congregations of archangels remained pristine. But then, as humans descended deeper into their avarice, into their heartlessness, they slaughtered archangels by the millions. And the beauteous geometry of heaven, the tendrils, the cusps, the roughness, the moistness, all venerable in its complexity, fell before the flat surfaces and right angles favored by the human conquerors.

"As the archangels fell, the angels perished. Where holy congregations once towered, where sacred choirs once sang, lifeless monuments were erected. And still the pace of the slaughter did not slacken. It intensified! And finally, one prophet saw that humans would soon be left alone with their lifeless monuments. And she cried out with a loud voice:

"'My brothers and sisters, see what we have become! In our rush to build lifeless monuments, we are exterminating the living archangels, who were built by one far greater than we! Even if we repent at once, thousands of years will pass before heaven heals itself of our violence! Let us feel the depth of our guilt! Let us feel the weight of our shame! We have lived as though we had no need of the archangels, so let us now prove it, by removing ourselves from their sight! We have lived as though we were above the archangels, so let us now place ourselves below them! We have demonstrated our unworthiness of living in heaven, so let us now cast ourselves into hell! We must fall into an abyss of our own creation to allow the greater creation to resurrect itself! As we suffer in the hellish depths, as we purge our heavy sins, our lifeless monuments will begin to crumble, and the archangels will spread once again across the face of heaven! And after all our lifeless monuments have vanished, after not one stone remains standing, only then may we turn our eyes toward the path of ascension back to heaven.'

"'And the humans hearkened to her words and wailed and beat their breasts and descended beneath heaven. Far below heaven, they built themselves a dungeon, a hell, a cube of 8,120,601 precincts in which to repent and purge themselves of sin.

"This creation myth has been called the philodendrist heresy. I've presented you with the standard version, but there are many variations, especially in the minor details. One variant differs significantly enough to be a heresy in its own right. I'll get to that later. There's also been significant debate over whether the philodendrist considered humans worthy of ever returning to heaven.

"Scholars identified three other heresies hidden in the troubadour ballads. The next one I'll tell you about is the warden heresy. The warden heresy lies at the core of all the others. A teaching cannot be heretical unless it has something to be heretical against. According to the warden heresy, a ruthless tyrant known as the warden is determined to keep the populace ignorant of the truth. It is the warden who propagates the great lie and persecutes those who expose it.

"The warden's power appears to be immense but not complete. If he had complete power, I would surely be dead, and even the troubadour ballads would have been obliterated from the libraries. So now we must ask ourselves: in what way is his power incomplete?

"Perhaps he fears that one of his minions plans to depose him and take his place. To prevent this, he must know each of his minions well. He must know their ambitions, their frustrations, and their deepest fears. He must know whom they love and where they live. This is a lot of information to acquire and keep track of, and he must do it all himself since he trusts no one. So he cannot have too many people working for him, and this severely limits his power. So he must make his foes into willing servants, as you say. He kills most of the heretics, but he leaves some terrorized survivors to spread blind panic, and this is how he suppresses interest in the heresies. Make sense?"

Danielle nodded. Her toes and fingers were going numb from the cold, but she was riveted in her seat.

"An alternative theory of the warden's limits has been put forward," Arlene continued. "Perhaps the warden's knowledge of the ancient secrets is incomplete. In this case, he is dependent on the heretics themselves to uncover the secrets. So does he let me live only to spread blind panic, or does he let me live to solve the final mysteries? I personally believe that it's both.

"The warden's identity is unknown. Many viewpoints have been articulated. Is the warden one man or many? Are there multiple wardens in competition with one another? Or multiple wardens who are not even aware of one another? Or is the warden heresy the invention of deranged scholars who murder their competitors? It's all a matter of conjecture.

"The next heresy is the entropy heresy. According to this heresy, no machine can last forever. Specifically, the machines that make our food, our water, and even our air will inevitably fail. Now, we do have machines that repair other machines, and there even are factories that make new machines. But now, look at the whole system of machines and factories. They all exist within the same six boundaries: $x = 1.00$, $x = -1.00$, $y = 1.00$, $y = -1.00$, $z = 1.00$, and $z = -1.00$. Nothing enters through these boundaries, and nothing leaves through them. And that means that the whole system contained within the boundaries is a kind of machine. And no machine can last forever. It will inevitably fail. And it cannot be melted down and replaced by some other machine because there is no other machine. The failure of the entire system may be immediate and catastrophic, or it may be gradual, even imperceptible, unless viewed over centuries. In any case, it is inevitable.

"The final heresy is the interment heresy. The interesting thing about this one is that it's heretical to the heretics. In other words, it contradicts not the great lie, but the philodendrist heresy. According to the interment heresy, most of the people in heaven were unmoved by the philodendrist's oratory. They liked living in heaven and did not want to leave. Some people shared the philodendrist's affection for the archangels, but even these people desired to remain with the archangels who still stood. So the philodendrist summoned up her weapons of war, great machines of fire and knifepoints. Some people battled against the machines, but these people fell, bloodied and maimed, before the bloodless enemy. So the rest of the people raised their hands in surrender, and with mighty sobs and lamentations, they left their beloved homes. Taking their wailing children by the hands, in darkness and in fear, with knifepoints at their backs, they descended into hell.

"It's a bit of historical irony that the interment heretics were persecuted worst of all—by the philodendrist heretics, who would not see their savior slandered! Only one troubadour dared encrypt the interment heresy in her ballads. She met a gruesome end that I'd rather not tell you about."

"It seems to me," Danielle said, "that the interment heresy is the least significant of the four since it has little relevance to our present predicament. What difference does it make now whether our forebears came here willingly or not?"

Arlene frowned. "The interment heresy is my personal specialty."

"I beg your pardon," Danielle said. "Please tell me more about it."

"I don't mind if I do," Arlene said. "There are some amusing rumors about Janet Peptide, the one scholar who encrypted the interment heresy. One scandalous rumor, which I believe to be true, is that she never had relations with fewer than five men at once. She was also rumored to demonstrate incredible mastery of her innards. She allegedly would go on stage, swallow a ball of yarn, and slowly excrete out a scarf. Her achievement is something I really aspire to."

"The scarf or the men?" Danielle asked.

"The scarf, of course," Arlene said. "I've already had the men. Who hasn't?"

Danielle raised her eyebrows.

"Don't worry," Arlene said. "You've got time. Anyway, this rumor's my favorite: when Janet Peptide stood on her head, she was able to see with her feet."

"I don't need eyes on my feet to see the silliness of these rumors," Danielle said. "And I think you're trying to distract me from things of importance. You're trying to deflect my interest from the unsettling facts, but it won't work."

Arlene nodded in admiration. "You're smarter than I thought," she said.

"I'm determined to see this through to the end," Danielle said. "So, we know that our forebears did not create the machines out of wisdom and love. Our forebears were sent here to suffer. And we're still suffering, for their sins, and the machines are breaking down, and we're all about to die, and an inaccessible world of happiness is somewhere high above us. What are we supposed to do now?"

Arlene gritted her teeth. "There are a few tiny little details that I haven't quite mentioned to you. These details are also extracted from the ballads, and they represent the very highest threat to the warden. If I communicate this information to you, the warden will know, and your life will never be the same. If you choose this path, unimaginable peril and persecution await you. You will be hunted from all sides without anyone to turn to. When you want to lie down, you will have to run, and when you want to run, you will be clamped in tight chains. You will be denied food when you are hungry and sleep when you are tired. Your pleas to return to your old life will earn you punishment, and your cries for mercy will be met by cruel laughter."

Danielle raised her shoulders. A strange exhilaration washed over her, and for a moment she forgot the chill. Her teeth were chattering and her whole body quivered, but she spoke fiercely. "I have leapt every obstacle placed before me," Danielle said. "I have triumphed over the worst that has come my way. Where others have failed, I will succeed. Where others whimper, I will roar. Where others cower, I will strike hard. Where others dawdle, I will hasten. Where others seek, I will hide, and labor undiscovered, until the prize is won!"

"Histrionics will not win you any prize," Arlene said. "The only thing that will help you is valor, and I see no evidence of it within you. I advise you to walk out while your legs are still able. This meeting is adjourned."

While speaking, Arlene rose and beckoned Danielle toward a door in the far corner. Following her lead, Danielle shouted, "You can't deter me from my search! I don't need you! When the new troubadours sing of my glory, you will be forgotten!"

Arlene put on the heavy coat and scarf that

hung on a rack by the door. She opened the door and skated through, beckoning Danielle onward. Danielle slid through the doorway and entered a small closet that was freezing cold. Spears of ice jutted from a duct along the wall. The duct jittered and clanked horribly. A layer of frost clung to the walls and ceiling. Danielle began to gasp at the cold, but the icy air caught in her throat and she choked. Arlene closed the door behind them.

"I hope you'll forgive my paranoia," Arlene said. "There are rumors that the warden has surveillance machines through which he sees and hears everything that happens. I personally believe these rumors to be false. I don't think such machines exist. But in case they do exist, I come in here, hoping that the cold and the noise will interfere with their operation."

Danielle began shivering uncontrollably. "Is that j-j-just an assumption? Or d-d-do you have any evidence that this c-c-cold offers s-s-some protection?"

Arlene shrugged. "It's just an assumption. But if you want to be some kind of champion, this is going to be the least of your challenges."

Danielle nodded. Her teeth were chattering so forcefully that her jaw ached.

"So," Arlene said, "the encrypted message in the ballads alludes to a passageway from hell back to heaven. A path of ascension. A path to be traveled by those who are worthy. But a path that is blocked to those who would repeat the crimes of our forebears. So of all the secrets, this is the very deepest, and it is encrypted the most elaborately of all.

"Now, we have to think geometrically. Out of the 8,120,601 precincts, which could connect to the path? All the interior precincts have adjacent precincts on all six sides, including the bottom and top. So the interior precincts cannot connect to a path directed elsewhere. But there are 40,401 precincts with $x = -1.00$, and at the far minus x edge of these precincts, there are 4,040,100 blocks that begin with A. Any one of these blocks could connect to the path, if the path happens to lead from the $x = -1.00$ side. But the path could lead from any of the other five sides of the cube of precincts. So there are approximately twenty-four million exterior blocks to which the path could connect. It would take lifetimes to explore all of them. So randomly choosing blocks is out of the question."

"Are you sure we should restrict our attention to exterior blocks?" Danielle said. "Couldn't a tunnel from an interior block go right through an exterior block, without opening into the exterior block?"

"That's true," Arlene said. "The path of ascension could begin in an interior block. But still, it couldn't help but penetrate an exterior block on its way out. So a careful search of the proper exterior block should reveal the path you describe. Agreed?"

Danielle nodded.

"It's possible, of course," Arlene continued, "that the ceiling of one block is far below the floor of the block above it. There could be a lot of empty space between blocks. And, in fact, there must be. Think of the enormous space required by the tunnels through which taxis travel. The tunnels connect every block in every precinct to all the rest. There must be an unimaginable number of intersections and ramps winding through the darkness. So you're right. An exhaustive search for the path of ascension should include not only the exterior blocks, but also the hidden spaces between exterior blocks."

"So where do we begin?" Danielle asked. The cold was seeping deeper into her body. Her stomach felt cold. The centers of her thighs felt cold.

"Only partial knowledge has been preserved," Arlene said. Her breath was visible as great white gusts. "Yet still, according to the encrypted message in the ballads, it is possible to determine which precinct connects to the path. Some people, alive today, have some knowledge pointing to the proper precinct. However, nobody's knowledge is complete. Some people may know the x coordinate, others may know the y coordinate, and still others may know the z coordinate.

What's worse is that the people who have this information probably don't even know what it is. They know nothing of the path of ascension or the philodendrist.

"We can imagine different ways in which this information is preserved. Perhaps some family has a tradition of playing a card game up to 71 points. No one remembers why 71 is the winning score, and no one cares. The rules for card games are always arbitrary. But not in this case. In this case, 71 is, let's say, the encrypted y coordinate, 0.71."

"But that's ridiculous!" Danielle said. "That's such a tenuous means of preserving the information! Some kid could change the winning score to 29, and no one would think anything of it, and then the encrypted information is corrupted!"

"That's why there are multiple layers of redundancy," Arlene said. "So, let's suppose, while this one family plays cards up to 71 points, another family in the same block likes to write poems with 71 syllables. And in another family in the same block, all the women with younger siblings live to the age of 71. So the encrypted message isn't just in traditions and ideas. It can be deeper than that. It can be in the blood."

"How is that possible?" Danielle asked. "Are you saying that something kills the women when they turn 71? Is it the medics? Is their food poisoned?

But that doesn't even make sense because most people don't live that long. Are these women given superior food? Superior treatment from the medics? Are they conscious of any secrets of longevity? Do they kill themselves at 71?"

"Any of these are possible," Arlene said, "as well as other possibilities we cannot even imagine. Perhaps something in their blood acts like a timer. We don't know how this timer was put in their blood. Perhaps you're right in supposing that the food machines and medics conspire to yield the desired outcome. This would have been established in forgotten antiquity. We don't know how it was done.

"Perhaps, too, the coordinates are encrypted in buildings or machines. Scuff marks on a doormat. Scratches on a window. The sputtering of a taxi as it rounds a corner. Any of these could hide the coordinates."

"Where do we look to find the coordinates?" Danielle asked.

"It is believed that the x coordinate is hidden in one block, the y coordinate is hidden in another block, and the z coordinate is hidden in a third block," Arlene said. "Unfortunately, no one knows the identity of these three blocks."

But she began writing with her finger in the frost: "X 0.38 -0.41 0.04 J3B." Danielle's eyes widened with understanding. The x coordinate was hidden in block J3B of precinct x = 0.38, y

= -0.41, z = 0.04. She carefully memorized this information.

Arlene spoke as she continued to write on the wall. "There are some secret networks of people who may have information unknown to scholars. Each cluster of people has its own agenda, and its own partial knowledge. Some people, like the warden, want to find the path of ascension in order to control it. Some want to travel it. Some want to destroy it. In any case, many of these people believe very strongly in some very strange things. The details aren't important, but stay away from the cult of the one eye. Those people have some screws loose."

Arlene finished writing on the wall: "Y -0.09 -0.11 -0.02 E4C. Z 0.20 0.18 0.16 C7B." Danielle memorized these numbers and letters as soon as they appeared. Arlene wiped her hand across the wall and erased everything.

"Finally," Arlene said, "I have three riddles. I extracted these from the troubadour ballads, but I don't know what they mean. The first is this: Look in only one eye."

Danielle's throat was so cold that she could not swallow. She was afraid that her saliva had frozen into a block of ice and was choking her. She took her trembling hands out of her pockets and began unwinding the scarf so that she could put it around her neck.

"The second is this," Arlene said. "Ice, ice, why, why twice?"

Danielle stretched open the scarf and glanced at the gashes on her hand. They were red and moist but no longer dripping. Arlene gasped, a sound that intensified to a shriek.

"The mark of the high heretic!" Arlene screamed, her eyes wild with panic. "Why have you come to doom me? They surely followed you here! Do you know what they'll do to me? I've already been warned!"

Arlene reached into her pocket and pulled out a gun.

"Is that a gun?" Danielle yelled. "I thought they only existed in myth!"

Danielle rushed to back away but slid on the ice and landed hard on her elbow. She groaned in pain and squirmed helplessly on the ice. Her heart raced, and her eyelids stretched open, as she imagined how a bullet would feel when it tore through her innards.

"I don't know who the high heretic is, but I assure you, it's not me!" Danielle pleaded. "I'm just a normal girl, unexceptional in every way, afflicted with chronic diarrhea! I never excelled at anything! Forget what I said about succeeding where others failed! I'll never say a word to anyone about what you told me!"

Arlene's lip curled in contempt. "Playing dumb might have fooled me, but it won't work on them." She raised the gun to her own head.

"No! Stop!" Danielle screamed.

Arlene pulled the trigger. Nothing happened.

"Unreliable piece of shit," Arlene said.

She pulled the trigger again. Danielle screamed, but Arlene fell silent.

5

Danielle did not know how long she lay sobbing on the ice. When she finally tried to move, all her joints were stiff, and her arms and legs were numb. Dragging her scarf, she crawled to the door. She pushed, but it did not budge. She did not see a doorknob or handle to pull. Her heart thumped, and she wondered if she would freeze to death in here. She rose shakily to her feet, leaning heavily on the wall. She slid her fingers along the chill edge of the door and found a small notch on the top. She slid in her finger, wrapped it around the door, and pulled the door open.

She stepped through and closed the door behind

her. She shook her arms and legs, grimacing at the stabbing pains that accompanied the return of sensation. She wiggled her jaw and rubbed her nose. Her lips were salty with tears. She wrapped the scarf back around her wounded hand.

She shambled over to a chair and sat, stupefied. She had spoken brave words, but when confronted with a gun, she panicked; when she witnessed sudden violence, she became hysterical. She needed to steel herself against the perils ahead. In fact, why should she prefer pleasure to pain? If this preference governed her behavior, then she was no better than a leisure carriage. Arlene had said that the only thing that would help her was valor. She resolved, therefore, to be valorous. No pain or threat of suffering would stop her.

She wondered if she should retrieve Arlene's gun. A rare, fearsome weapon promised to be useful. However, she knew nothing about how to use it. She was afraid that it would accidently fire in her pocket and maim her. Arlene had carried it in her pocket, but Arlene may have taken some precaution that Danielle did not know about. Also, if the gun were effective against the enemy, then Arlene would have chosen to live and defend herself. Danielle decided to leave the gun with Arlene.

Danielle was now the heir, perhaps the sole heir, to the archeolinguists' scholarship. The path of ascension began somewhere, and

Danielle knew where to search for each of the three coordinates. She mentally reviewed the information that Arlene had written in the frost. The hiding place for the y coordinate was closest, in the E4C block of precinct $x = -0.09$, $y = -0.11$, $z = -0.02$. Danielle would go there now.

She opened the door to the hallway and peered outside. A lanky man wearing ice skates coasted up and down the hallway. Danielle stared at him with suspicion. He looked at her quizzically.

With a spray of ice, he braked in front of her. "Are you alright?" he asked.

"I don't know," Danielle answered. "I've had better days. How do I look?"

"Inquisitive," he said. "Fierce. Endearingly petulant."

"That's what people say when I ask," Danielle said, "which is why I ask as often as I can. It's a kind of technique I have for boosting my morale."

"That's a clever technique," the man said. "You're bright as well as beautiful."

"Thank you," Danielle said. "Thank you for brightening my day. Well. I'll be on my way."

She took a step and slid on the ice, nearly losing her balance.

"This ice is driving me crazy!" she said.

"Ice, ice, why, why twice?" asked the man.

Danielle gulped. "What do you know?" she said. "Who are you?"

The man skated swiftly away.

"Come back!" Danielle said, scampering after him. But she had to go slowly to keep her balance; she did not want any more bruises than she already had. By the time Danielle reached the end of the hall, the man was nowhere to be seen.

Danielle went toward the main doors of the library. A pregnant woman sat at a table and read. Two old men leaned over a manuscript and argued quietly, wagging their fingers in each other's faces. No one seemed aware of the menace that had terrorized Arlene and poisoned Jerry. Danielle felt envy and yet also a strange pity for the people uninvolved in her struggle.

Danielle left the library. Skaters whisked every which way. A man, balanced on a large ball, juggled three miniature unicycles. He drew a small crowd of admirers. A maintenance vehicle lumbered down the street, smoothing the ice with a great spinning disk.

"Taxi," Danielle called.

Two old women and an old man shuffled by, walking with canes. The old man leaned into Danielle's ear and said, "Take heed. You have many enemies."

"Who are you?" Danielle said. "Come back! Wait! Stop!"

She followed him and put her hand on his shoulder. He spun around and struck his cane against her knee. She gasped at the pain.

"Let me go!" he shouted. "Stop following me!"

People stared. Danielle looked around and saw puzzled, disapproving faces. She blushed deeply.

"I—I'm sorry," Danielle said. "I mistook you for someone else. Please, forgive me."

People walked on. Danielle waited awkwardly, casting frequent, nervous glances behind her. The taxi arrived, and Danielle got in. The safety belt slithered around her waist and clicked into the buckle.

"The E4C block of precinct x = -0.09, y = -0.11, z = -0.02," she said.

The taxi meandered through the crowd toward the tunnel entrance. Danielle noticed a piece of paper wedged into the seat beside her. She lifted and unfolded it. "Turn back or die," it read.

Danielle looked frantically in all directions. She felt trapped in the safety belt. Nothing unusual was visible inside the taxi. Out on the street, typical skaters and musicians mulled about. No one seemed to be paying any attention to Danielle. The taxi entered the tunnel.

"Are you listening?" Danielle shouted in the darkness. "I'm unstoppable. Your hollow threats betray your fear. You know you can't beat me! Why do you even try? You're wasting your time! You have no power over me!"

Shrouded in the blackness of the tunnel, Danielle's shoulders heaved and her cheeks were soaked with tears.

6

Danielle calmed herself before the taxi emerged from the tunnel. She stepped out of the taxi near a factory. Motorized carts full of plastic chairs, tablecloths, and clothes entered one door. Carts full of books emerged from a second door. Danielle supposed that the chairs, tablecloths, and clothes were recycled into books.

Danielle examined the scene, searching for anything that could possibly represent the secret y coordinate. The stacks of books differed in height from cart to cart. She did not think that each cart contained the same number of books. She guessed that each book had more than 100 pages; she could not imagine how a number greater than 100 could represent a coordinate from -1.00 to 1.00.

Danielle walked down the street. She passed a restaurant, a gym, and two apartment buildings. The pedestrians that she passed appeared totally ordinary. Children rode bicycles, old women sat on benches, and one shaggy man walked on stilts. Then one young woman hurried past Danielle and whispered, "You're getting closer. Take heart!"

"Please!" Danielle said, trotting after the woman. "Why did you tell me this? What is your purpose?"

"I say this to every stranger I see," the woman said. "My boxing instructor told me to. I'm not sure why. I think it helps distract me from my bruises."

"Could you introduce me to your boxing instructor?" Danielle asked.

"No," the woman said. "He told me that you'd ask, and he told me to say no."

"He told you about me, specifically? About someone who looks just like me?"

The woman nodded. "He said that if you asked these follow-up questions, then I definitely shouldn't take you to him."

"Then could you walk with me, just for a little while?" Danielle said. "I'm feeling—I'm feeling very alone. I've heard so many distressing things today. I don't know why so many people know who I am and where I'm going. I think it would really help me feel stronger if I could have someone beside me, at least for a little while."

The woman punched Danielle in the mouth. Danielle winced forcefully and bled from her lips.

"I'm sorry," the woman said. "My boxing instructor said you'd block that if you had any chance of succeeding in your search. I'm sorry. You're not the one. I have to go."

Danielle's eyes watered, and she couldn't see where the woman went. Danielle wiped her eyes and walked into the nearest restaurant. She got in line behind the water dispenser. When it was her turn, she absently said, "Temperature 0.7." She took her glass of water and sat at a table. She coughed at orange vapors and dabbed at her lip with her scarf.

She thought about what the woman boxer had told her. Maybe there was some kind of encoded message. Maybe the message was to remain alert and vigilant at all times. Danielle must never again let her guard down.

She left the restaurant and expanded her defensive awareness to everything around her. Were there second-floor windows from which someone could drop something on her head? Was anyone within striking range of her? Was anyone carrying something that could be thrown at her? Were any vehicles moving toward her? Could she hear any vehicles in the distance? Was anyone reaching for a gun? Was she in anyone's line of sight? Could anyone be hiding behind something, or around a corner? She resolved to maintain this level of awareness always.

She continued vigilantly down the street. She came to a park. Many children sat on the ground and played with jigsaw puzzles. The puzzles looked very difficult. All the pieces were uniformly black. The goal seemed to be to arrange the pieces in a square.

Danielle glanced from one child's puzzle to the next. All the puzzles appeared identical. Her pulse quickened. Perhaps the number of puzzle pieces was the clue she needed. She attempted to count the number of pieces in one puzzle, but with the pieces constantly moving around, it was impossible to keep track of which pieces she had already counted.

"Excuse me," she said to a pudgy boy. "May I try your puzzle for just a minute?"

"Okay," he said. "I'm practicing for the competition. It's a race. You have to put the puzzle together as fast as you can."

"I see," Danielle said, sitting down.

She began to count the pieces. When she counted a piece, she pushed it to the side.

"No, that's not where it goes," the boy said. "Why are you putting the pointy pieces near the curvy pieces? Here, let me help you."

"No, that's okay, I can do it myself," Danielle

said, but the boy was already rearranging the pieces.

"Can't you see that this one curves out exactly how that one curves in?" the boy said. "And this one is way too big to fit in here. And that piece—"

"Please! I want to try this myself!" Danielle said, attempting to reverse what the boy was doing. "How am I going to get any practice if you do it all for me?"

"But I'm helping you practice to improve your speed," the boy said. "If you practice going super slow, you just get really good at going super slow."

"Will you just keep your hands off the puzzle for one minute?" Danielle snapped.

"Gee lady," the boy said. "You sure are a grouch."

"Wait until you get to be my age," Danielle said. "Then you'll understand."

"I don't think I'll live that long," the boy said. "People in my family die before they're 50."

"Just keep your mouth shut, will you?" Danielle said.

The boy began humming loudly. Danielle glared at him, but he just smiled and hummed more loudly. Danielle turned back to the puzzle and counted the pieces. There were 43.

"Okay, I give up," Danielle said. "You can have your puzzle back."

"I didn't think you could possibly be as stupid as you are grouchy," the boy said, "but you sure proved me wrong."

"Get used to it," Danielle said.

Danielle stomped toward a bench and sat down. Could $y = 0.43$ be the coordinate she sought here? Arlene had said that there was redundancy in the preservation of the coordinates. So the number 43 should recur in other forms in this block.

Danielle glanced around the park. Many people were sitting on benches and watching the children solve their puzzles. Three bald men sat on the bench right in front of her. Something made her stare at the backs of their heads. Each of them had a small number of short hairs near the base of the skull. She wanted to count the hairs, but she needed to get closer. She approached the men.

"Excuse me," she said, "but I'm a dabbler in a rare form of scalp massage. Hair, to me, is a terribly vexing obstruction, and I couldn't help but notice that you gentlemen are unencumbered. May I request permission to practice my art form on your scalps?"

The three men looked at one another hesitantly.

"Just don't tell our wives!" blurted one, and they all laughed.

Danielle sighed in relief and stepped behind the first man. She kneaded his scalp mindlessly as she counted his hairs. Forty-three. She repeated this with the two other men. Each had 43 hairs.

"Thank you, gentlemen," Danielle said. "I relish

every opportunity to practice my art."

"You really have a knack," said one of the men.

"A talent," said the second.

"You are an incomparable gift to mankind," said the third. "Say, what happened to your face?"

"Ice skating accident," Danielle said.

"That's a relief," the man said. "I was afraid you had a lot of enemies! Anyways, take good care of yourself."

"I will," Danielle said.

She walked away, troubled by his words. She tried to put it out of her mind. Now was time to celebrate. She had confirmed one of the three coordinates! Only two remained. This seemed too easy.

She wandered back toward the tunnel door. The z coordinate was hidden in the C7B block of $x = 0.20$, $y = 0.18$, $z = 0.16$. She would go there next. She decided to save the x coordinate for last because it was hidden further away.

Then she remembered something. The pudgy boy had said that no one in his family lived to be 50. Could it be that they lived to be 43? If so, she would have additional confirmation of the y coordinate. She turned around to look for the boy.

But she had forgotten to be vigilant. A man with a long, blond braid had been following her. He slammed his fist into her stomach.

"Turn back or die," he said.

Danielle's stomach imploded, and she crumpled

to the ground. A wrenching spasm tore through her innards, and she simultaneously vomited and discharged diarrhea. Danielle gagged at the odor and coughed painfully.

"Medic," she whimpered.

She gasped and tried to cancel the medic request, but her throat produced no sound. Through half-closed eyes, she saw a needle extend from a red hose into her right elbow, and into the darkness she slid.

7

A single wisp of white vapor rises through the darkness. A second white tendril ascends. The two spiral each other coyly. Additional white vapor billows upward, gathering, gushing, until a bright cloud churns against the darkness. Then the center of the cloud opens, and through the wispy opening, Danielle sees herself, clad in an unfamiliar tunic. A fierce wind disperses the white vapor, and the tunic-clad Danielle marches onward. Her calves are taut, and her feet are bare. She walks along a narrow ledge between a deep pit and rough, stone wall.

She follows a man who wears smooth, tan

pants and many pouches on his belt. Slung over one shoulder is a long, curved rod whose ends are connected by a taut string. Over his other shoulder is a narrow, cylindrical basket containing long sticks with strangely decorated ends. He wears no shirt, and he is more muscular than anyone Danielle has ever seen. He would surely triumph in any athletic contest. His scalp is bald, and his beard is thick, curly, and black. His lips curl in a slight grin. He wears a blindfold. He is walking backwards, and with each step, he places his foot so that half of it extends over the ledge.

"Cougar, please walk normally," Danielle says. "You're frightening me."

"Lest the people starve, a hunter must always practice poise," he responds. "And if this frightens you, then everything will. You must learn courage."

Danielle snorts defiantly. She turns around and closes her eyes. She slides one foot backwards until it extends over the ledge. She lifts her other foot. She smiles in exhilaration, but then she sways slightly, and her brain seems to slosh in her skull. She is not sure which direction is up. Panicked, she opens her eyes, but she is already falling. Her face is level with her knees. She flails her arms but cannot reach the ledge. Then Cougar's hand catches her wrist. He hoists her into his arms.

"Courage does not mean recklessness," he says. "I have trained in poise since childhood. I can teach you what I know. You can learn to do what I do. But not if your recklessness kills you first."

"Your feet are still hanging off the edge, and you're still wearing your blindfold!" Danielle exclaims, clinging to his shoulders. "How were you able to catch me?"

"You can learn to do what I do," he repeats, perhaps with a hint of weariness. "I am able to carry you. I hardly feel your weight. But would you prefer to walk on your own feet?"

"Yes," Danielle says, drawing a deep, ragged breath. "Okay. I'm ready. Put me down!"

Cougar smiles. "I have already taught you much of the art of grappling," he says. "You must earn your own release."

"But if I knock you off balance, we'll both fall and die!" Danielle says.

Cougar laughs. "Would you rather live captive, or die fighting for your freedom?"

Danielle roars in challenge. She wedges her elbow against Cougar's throat and hurls her weight against it. Simultaneously, she slides her foot behind Cougar's knee and stomps. Cougar releases Danielle and falls into a backwards somersault.

"Not bad," he says. "In a real combat situation, you should have pushed me off the ledge, not away from it. I know you were concerned for my safety, but you needn't be. My skills are so much more advanced than yours."

"Some day that pride is going to lay you low," Danielle says.

"And until that day comes, I'll believe it never will," Cougar laughs. "Now come, we have little daylight remaining, and I want to show you something. But we must ascend further, and the air will be harder to breathe. Do you think you will be able to adjust?"

"Since childhood, I have trained in breathing air that's hard to breathe," Danielle smirks. "I'll find some merit yet in my upbringing."

Cougar removes his blindfold and smiles, blinking beneath the brilliant, blue ceiling. "I never supposed that one of the crypt-born could be so lovely," he says.

He resumes walking backwards along the edge, and Danielle follows. They ascend steeply. A dull throb builds in Danielle's head.

"Are we ascending to the great fire in the sky?" she gasps.

"No," Cougar says. "We believe that the great fire is high above the range of arrows, even arrows fired from the highest mountain peak. Even so, we are forbidden to fire arrows at it, lest we wound it and send it roaring from the sky. Many young warriors boast that they would be able to strike it, were they allowed."

"I'm sure you boasted loudest of all," Danielle says.

"You speak truly, Danielle Gasket," Cougar says. He smiles, but his dark brown eyes are wary, never resting long on any sight. He walks backwards quickly, each foot landing securely on the ledge's edge. Danielle glances into the gigantic pit beside them. Below some lingering white mist, there is an incalculable distance to the rocky floor. The rocks look sharp and hard, perfect for shattering skulls and splintering ribs.

"How can you stand to live in constant peril?" Danielle asks, stepping unsteadily with her hands against the cold, stone wall.

"There is always peril," Cougar answers. "Sometimes it's obvious, sometimes it's not. I prefer the obvious kind."

He looks into the pit and then grins at Danielle. He leans sideways over the pit, feigns a horrified expression, and begins to fall. His feet come off the ledge, and he drops, but then he catches the ledge with one hand. Squeezing his great biceps, he springs upward and lands silently on one foot. With a crooked smile, Danielle claps slowly. Cougar lavishly bows. They continue their ascent.

"We have some knowledge of the crypt nation," Cougar says. "We do not know how we came upon this knowledge. Perhaps, in the forgotten past, some of our people explored the crypt nation. Or, perhaps, one of our prophets beheld it in a vision. Or you are not the first to ascend. In any case, we are told that you have symbols that represent the sounds of speech. Is this true?"

"Yes," Danielle gasps. She leans against the wall and pauses to catch her breath. The air is thin, and Cougar walks quickly. The ledge has grown very narrow, scarcely the width of her foot. Ahead, Cougar balances on his toes on the narrowest point of the ledge, where it is only two inches wide.

"Cougar, I can't go on," Danielle says. "The ledge is too thin for me. I'm sorry. I can hardly keep my weight on the ledge even where I am. It feels like the wall itself is trying to push me off."

"You don't have to go any further," Cougar says. "We're here. Look. Do you recognize these symbols?"

Cougar points to the wall directly above his head. Many small symbols are chiseled into the stone.

"I—I think so," Danielle says. "It looks like writing. I'm too far away. I have to get closer."

Pressing her chest flat against the wall, she shuffles slowly toward Cougar. Even with her toes touching the wall, her heels extend off the ledge. Her eyelids flutter, and she clenches her teeth.

"If I blink too hard, the gust will blow me off the ledge," she says. "Cougar, you have no idea how hard this is for me. We don't have anything like this in the crypt nation."

"It would be a pity if you fall now, having come so close," Cougar says, still balanced on his toes without touching the wall. "We call this the silent stone because we cannot hear its speech. I was hoping you would open the lips of the silent stone."

Danielle presses her body hard against the wall. The stone is cold against her cheekbone. She breathes shallowly, as each expansion of her chest pushes her away from the wall. She extends an arm towards Cougar.

"Cougar, take my hand," Danielle says.

Cougar sighs and looks away. He lifts one foot from the ledge and rotates his ankle languidly.

"Please, Cougar! I need you!" Danielle says. She trembles, and tears gather in her eyes.

"This isn't a game anymore!" Danielle shouts. "You win! You're better than I! I'm just a worthless crypt-born, a burden to your people! Now take me home! I'll return to the crypt nation, if that's what you want!"

Balanced on three toes, Cougar pulls a knife from a sheath and begins trimming the toenails on his raised foot. He ignores Danielle.

"If this is how much you care about me, then I'm sorry I ascended!" Danielle cries. "Goodbye, Cougar! I'm going home!"

She pushes hard against the stone and falls backwards off the ledge. Cougar has to leap off after her, catching her wrist in one hand and the ledge in the other. He somehow has time to sheathe his knife first. He breathes heavily, and

Danielle dangles and sobs.

"Such histrionics!" Cougar says. "The crypt-born clearly surpass us in theater! I'll never again claim that we are superior in all things!"

Danielle laughs through her tears. With a grunt, Cougar lifts Danielle's hand to the ledge. She raises her other hand and claws the ledge with her fingers.

"Can you hang on for just a moment?" Cougar asks.

Danielle nods. Cougar pulls himself up onto the ledge. He faces the silent stone and balances on his toes. He lets his feet slide away from each other until he is doing a split along the ledge. Even though his torso is vertical, his nose almost touches the wall because the ledge is so narrow. His extends his arms behind his hips and grabs Danielle's wrists. He pulls his legs back together, sliding his feet along the ledge.

"Climb up onto my shoulders," he instructs Danielle. "You'll need to stand to see the highest symbols."

Danielle dangles limply from his arms and rests her head against his thighs.

"How do you have such supernatural strength?" she asks.

"It's not supernatural; it's natural," he says. "It's so natural that perhaps it is, as you say, super natural. You can learn to do what I do."

Danielle bends her arms until she can put her

feet on the ledge. She repositions her hands, one at a time, from Cougar's hands to his shoulders. She presses down on his shoulders, lifting her feet to his hips. He steadies her feet with his hands as she leans against the stone and straightens her legs. Pressing her hands against the chiseled stone, she steps up onto Cougar's shoulders. She looks down and sees that Cougar is still balanced on his toes without touching the wall.

"Well?" Cougar says. "Do you recognize the symbols?"

Danielle shifts her hands to find where the inscription begins. She begins to laugh. Her knees quake against the stone.

"What's so funny?" Cougar asks, frowning.

"It's doggerel!" Danielle says. "We're both about to plummet to our deaths, just for doggerel!"

"Well, I'd still like to hear it," Cougar says indignantly. "These are the only surviving symbols from the time of the philodendrist. Someone had a reason for inscribing them here."

"Okay," Danielle says. "Well, this seems to be a collection of writings. It's called The Doggerel of Janet Peptide. An ancient crypt-born poet went by the same name; maybe she somehow knew of these inscriptions. The first inscriptions are songs. There are musical symbols above the words, but I never learned how to sing. I cannot interpret the musical symbols."

"Just try, Danielle Gasket," Cougar says. "Try

to sing these songs as they were sung before the interment."

"Okay, but I'm going to have to make up the melody. This first song is called The Song of the Mountain Lion."

"That's remarkable!" Cougar exclaims. "The angel from which I take my name is sometimes called mountain lion."

"Oh!" Danielle says. "Then maybe this song is about you! Here it goes. Wait! Could you snap your fingers to give me some kind of beat? Great. Thanks.

"I drink from the river, watch the stars shiver in waves that circle my tongue. My jaws make a doe fall, the sound of a snowfall, a song in whispers sung.

"I growl if I have to, prowl if I have to, run with the storm cloud's speed. I fight if I have to, bite if I have to, bleed if I have to bleed.

"I wait if I have to, mate if I have to, bring young into my den. With eyes full of wonder, and throat full of thunder, I roar, and roar again.

"I purr if I have to, lick fur if I have to, teach the forest's joys. I know that I have to show that they have to bound without a noise.

"The trees are now fallen. The boulders are calling my kind to our final rest. And you're left alone with a mountain of bone that sinks in our mother's breast.

"I sigh if I have to, cry if I have to, grieve if I have

to grieve. I roared when I got to, soared when I got to, I leave when I have to leave."

Danielle licks her lips. The air here is dry.

"You spoke truly, Danielle Gasket, when you said that you have not learned how to sing," Cougar says.

Danielle laughs. "That's a sad song," she says. "Did all the mountain lions die?"

"No!" Cougar says. "They prosper to this day! Back where the ledge was wider, I saw many of their tracks. I will show them to you when we return. I know that you saw nothing."

"Maybe I can't read tracks, but I can read these songs," Danielle retorts. "Do you want me to continue?"

"Please," Cougar says.

"The next one is called The Griffin of Ragnarok. Is a griffin another kind of angel?"

"I know of no such angel," Cougar says, "but there are other lands beyond the great waters. We hear that the angels there are different. Perhaps one of these distant lands is called Ragnarok."

"Or maybe," Danielle says, "the griffin wasn't as lucky as the mountain lion. In any case, this is the song.

"Astride all his treasure, wealth beyond measure, the griffin of Ragnarok guards his nest. Piles of silver, tall as a hill, for only the griffin's claws to caress.

"For more than a century the griffin stood

sentry over the envy of a thousand kings. Moss is his diet. Alone in his quiet, the griffin decides it's time to stretch his wings.

"He mounts to the sky, rolls in delicate spirals, scanning the mountainside—is something wrong? No hawks shriek in greeting. No wrens flee, retreating. No warblers embrace the dawn with their song.

"No elk sniff the breezes. No porcupine squeezes beneath fallen branches where the shade is dark. No rabbits are dashing. No otters are splashing. No beavers are biting down through the bark.

"And down on the beaches, no sandpiper screeches. No crab scuttles with the waves. No tortoise crawls. No sharks swarm the basin. No eels find their place in cold, sandy blankets where the blackness falls.

"Towns that were beside mountains or seaside are now heaps of rubble laced with moss and vines. Winds blow the shards of glass through the yards thick with brambles and goldenrod and swaying pines.

"With a lump in his chest, he returns to his nest, which no longer seems to be a lofty throne. Did thousands of kings envy the wrong things? The griffin is pondering, all alone.

"Astride all his treasure, wealth beyond measure, the griffin of Ragnarok guards his nest. Piles of silver, tall as a hill, for only the griffin's claws to caress."

A cold wind rasps across the mountainside, and Danielle presses her feet into Cougar's shoulders. Her wrists and calves are tight from balancing against the stone.

"I do not think any of that really happened," Cougar says. "All the angels that the griffin sought still thrive. But perhaps they were not thriving at the time of the interment. What is the next song?"

"It's called The Hunt of the Werewolves. I think you'll like it. It's very ferocious!

"On starlit nights, we hunt our prey, the cunning werewolves, which we'll slay with arrows swift from bowstrings taut. Mighty battles will be fought.

"Our torches light the haunted fens. We search for signs of werewolf dens. Each shadow makes a panting sound. Werewolves must be all around.

"On moonlit nights, we leap and howl and look for men to disembowel. In this wood where darkness hangs, they will know the grip of fangs.

"And from our throats our fury pries the ragged hunger of our cries. Our tongues scrape thorns but feel no pains and crave the warmth of human brains.

"And we, on starlit nights, give thanks for songs of spears in werewolf flanks. We stomp the mud and burn the shrubs as though they crept with werewolf cubs.

"The hunt draws on along the heath, and torchlight glimmers on our teeth. We snarl and spit, as though we clothe our faces with the beasts we loathe.

"And we, on moonlit nights, grind stones between our teeth like human bones. We drag our snouts through dust and ooze. Our quarry leave a thousand clues.

"Thirsting for the coming fight, our frenzied wailing floods the night. We rise on hind legs with a grunt, as though we mock the thing we hunt.

"On starlit nights, we never doubt that werewolves must be all about. Werewolves, come! Be not afraid! End this now upon the blade!

"On moonlit nights, we shriek and hate the empty grasping of the wait. Humans, why prolong your fright? Our jaws will guide you into night!

"And they, until they end the rage that drags them in a shifting cage, beneath the moon, each month, transform! Self-chased like snow within a storm."

"I have heard," Cougar says, "that across the great waters there are people with the power to take the forms of angels. I do not know if this is true."

"You've never crossed the great waters?" Danielle says.

"No," Cougar says. "The journey is seldom made, and never by my own people. Generations ago, large, floating vessels appeared on the great waters. My people hid in the forest on the other side of the salt marsh. The vessels came ashore, and the visitors stepped out onto the moist and crumbling sand. These visitors gathered driftwood to make fire, and they set up their camp. Night fell, and they laughed and sang merrily around their fires. They drank fragrant tea from clay mugs. In the darkness, our greatest scouts, invisible like the wind, crept into the visitors' camp. The visitors continued laughing and carousing. Our scouts searched the entire camp but could not find any weapons. They searched the anchored vessels as well, but they found little more than stone urns holding water and smoked fish.

"Now, one of the scouts that night was the greatest in my people's history. Her name was Anemone. Like a shadow, she crept silently upon the visitors. While the visitors clapped and sang and tended their fires, Anemone's fingers, like tendrils of smoke, explored the visitors' pockets. She searched the pockets of 43 visitors, and she found nothing but herbs and harmless wooden figurines. All the while, the visitors continued singing, slapping each other on the back, and belching loudly.

"Then, Anemone reached into the pocket of the final visitor, an old man with long, white braids. She nearly pricked her fingers on a sharp, stone knife. She stealthily slid the knife from the visitor's pocket as he hummed and squinted at the fire. Upon sand, pebbles, and seaweed, she crept silently away, but after only several paces, her eyes widened in astonishment. She reached for the knife at her belt, but she found the sheath empty. She stared, bewildered, at the knife in her hand. She had thought that she stole the visitor's knife, but in fact, he had stolen hers!

"The visitors all roared with laughter. 'Come, join us, little sister!' the old man cried. 'As well as your seven friends who pretend to be unseen!'

"Shaken, the scouts stepped out of the shadows and humbly approached the visitors. They feasted all night on smoked fish and hallucinogenic tea. The next day, the scouts and the visitors exchanged gifts and kind words, and the visitors departed, never to return. From time to time, my people speak of the visitors and contemplate a journey across the great waters. But our vessels are small, and the waters are rough, and most importantly, we are happy here and do not wish to leave."

"I think the real reason," Danielle snickers, "is that you can't stand to be around people who are clearly your superiors!"

"And you, on the other hand, clearly have no such qualms!" Cougar laughs.

"I'll give you a point for wit," Danielle says, "but I'd like to see you survive in the crypt nation."

"Perhaps you will," Cougar sighs.

"What do mean?" Danielle says. "Why would we want to go there?"

"Never mind," Cougar says. "Sing me the next song."

"Oh. Alright," Danielle says, shifting her feet on Cougar's shoulders. "I should know better than to think I'll ever get away from ominous riddles. This next song is A Hawk Screeches Twice.

"Barn owls on the rafters are humming low, and all the hay bales in the stable are hiding mice, and near the turnips in the garden a tortoise crawls, and past the thunderclouds a hawk screeches twice.

"I'm ready to sprout out of the ground into the sky. I'm filling my sacks with feathers and corn, apples and rye. I'm sweeping the hall, shaking the rugs, shutting the door. I'm smelling the thyme, wondering if I'll smell it once more.

"Masts are creaking as the winds tear the sails, and all the raindrops pelt my forehead and coat the deck, and from the starboard side a wave crashes through the rails, and now I'm wondering if I'll live through the wreck.

"I swim through the night, clutching a plank, kicking through waves. Skulls, below on the sand, rolling with tides, call from their graves. Dawn comes with the fog, colder than ice, hiding the shore. I pull back my hair, wondering if I'll touch it once more.

"Here upon the tower, I smooth my robes and call the lightning to the amethyst in my hands, and all the wizards smile and say I've passed my test, but round the tower stretch the lone, level sands.

"I'm ready to swoop out of the sky onto the earth. I've searched all the stars but can't find a thing that has greater worth. I land on the sand, roll on my back, let out a roar. I glance at the tower, wondering if I'll come back once more."

Danielle straightens her spine and rotates her shoulders. She has read the upper inscriptions, and she now must stoop to continue reading.

"Can you squat down a little?" Danielle says. "If it doesn't endanger our lives any further? Otherwise, I'll have to sit on your shoulders to read the next song."

"I think you'll be more comfortable if you sit on my shoulders," Cougar says. "I can see your calves trembling with exertion."

"Okay," Danielle says.

She stoops and grabs Cougar's smooth forehead. She slides one foot, then the other, down his shoulders and around his ribs. She glimpses the mist in the pit behind them, and she sways dizzily. She squeezes Cougar's head with her thighs.

"I'm sorry," she says. "I'm just trying not to fall off. Can you still hear me?"

"Yes," Cougar says. "My hearing is very acute. And this is rather pleasant. My ears were starting to get cold."

He remains balanced on his toes upon the tiny

ledge. Danielle shakes her head admiringly.

"Okay," Danielle says. "The next song is called Comparison.

"I fished beside the restless tide and blessed my happy fate: honest neighbors, easy labors, fish to bite my bait. Faithful friends and gentle bays, I fished through many happy days.

"The king rode down in golden crown to take his regal tour. Embroidered hems and gorgeous gems informed me: I was poor. My house, my boat, my other things—so much cruder than the king's.

"I fish beside the restless tide and curse my wretched fate: heavy oars, unwelcome doors to poverty and hate. Now, I know. I mourn. I grieve. At least, no more am I naïve."

"And yet," Cougar says, "the fisherman has actually become more ignorant of the simple joys all around him."

Danielle's hands are cold against the stone. Squeezing Cougar's head with her thighs, she brings her hands to her mouth and blows on them. Her breath feels cold and thin, and her hands do not warm.

"There's only one more song," Danielle says. "After this, there are some fables and some kind of philosophical rambling. Then, the final bit is called a prayer, whatever that means. I won't be sorry when we finish reading. I'm starting to get cold."

"Then go on," Cougar says. "Sing me the last song."

"Okay," Danielle said. "Here it is.

"There are cars in the lot. Now there's mine in its spot, but there's one thing it's not: there is nothing alive. It's the end of my ride. There's a curb on the side, but you really can't hide: there is nothing alive.

"On my desk there's a screen, and it has a nice sheen because I keep it quite clean. There is nothing alive. We have eight plastic plants, and they don't attract ants. They really don't stand a chance. There is nothing alive.

"People shop in their marts, and there's cans in their carts, but I look in their hearts, and there's nothing alive. As the earth mother dies, hardly anyone cries, and I look in their eyes, and there's nothing alive."

8

Danielle awoke on the ground. She blinked and rolled her head. The street was oddly deserted. She sat up. Her head spun, but only briefly. She nervously pressed her fingers against her stomach. She felt no pain, just a slight numbness that was dissolving into small prickles. She pressed lower against her abdomen. Even there, the familiar aches were milder than usual. Something was very strange. She gasped. There was no trace of vomit on her clothing, and no stench of diarrhea. Was it normal for a medic to bathe her and wash her clothing while she wore it?

Whatever had happened to her, she felt better now than just before the blow to her stomach. The ache in her wounded hand had subsided. She looked beneath the scarf wrapped around her hand. The gashes were clean, dry, and neatly scabbed. The bruises on her cheek and elbow were less tender than before, and her punched lip was much less swollen. How many injuries she had sustained lately! Her heart swelled with pride. A warrior is proud of her scars.

Then she noticed a scratchy pain in her right forearm. She did not remember having any injuries there. She pulled up the sleeve of her jacket and gaped at her new tattoo: "Turn back or die, bitch." She was too proud of her warrior status to feel dismayed.

"A warrior is proud of her scars!" she shouted. "Your petty efforts to dissuade me only buoy me onward!"

She surveyed the street carefully. She had twice been caught off guard. If it happened again, the next time could end with a knife instead of a fist. She renewed her vow of constant vigilance. She could not afford to fail again.

She heard footsteps from a side street. She stood up and assumed a defensive posture. A bald man appeared. He broke into a smile.

"Hey, magic fingers!" he said. "How about a scalp massage?"

Danielle grinned.

"Okay," she said, "while I wait for a taxi. Taxi!"

As she kneaded his scalp, she kept a careful watch on her surroundings. Several children ran by, chasing a ball. A young couple bickered while strolling hand in hand. Danielle tried to remain conscious of every detail. When the taxi approached, she made sure that it was decelerating properly. She scoped out an entrance to a warehouse where she would flee if the vehicle tried to run her down.

She gave the bald scalp a final pat and examined the taxi before stepping inside.

"Thanks a bundle!" the man said. "Just please don't tell my wife!"

"Don't worry," Danielle said. "I've become something of a specialist in secrecy."

9

Danielle arrived in the C7B block of precinct x = 0.20, y = 0.18, z = 0.16. Here, she would search for the hidden z coordinate. The taxi stopped in front of a cluster of stationary bicycles. The people pedaling the bicycles were simultaneously playing trumpets. Half a dozen children jumped up and down to the beat.

Danielle got out of the taxi. There were a lot of vehicles and pedestrians on the road. Danielle did her very best to remain aware of them all as she casually glanced around. One woman had a long knife and carved a block of plastic as she walked. She paid no attention to Danielle, nor to where she was walking. She frequently bumped into the wall. Danielle felt safe, but she kept her guard up.

Danielle began her search for the z coordinate. She counted the number of stationary bicycles. There were 13, but two were unoccupied. There were three valves on each trumpet. No number was asserting itself yet.

A tall woman walked through the crowd and handed out origami tetrahedrons. Most of the recipients were indifferent or annoyed. As Danielle opened her hand to receive it, she readied her other hand to deflect a blow or to counterattack. She had her back angled toward a wall to make sure that no one crept up behind her.

The tall woman gave Danielle a tetrahedron and walked on. Danielle unfolded it, frequently glancing away to maintain her vigilance. Written on the paper was the message, "You're getting closer. Take heart!"

Danielle looked toward the woman, who was now many paces away. The woman stared right at Danielle and then turned and fled. Danielle gave chase.

Danielle circumvented a marching string quartet and nearly collided with an old man.

"So sorry," Danielle gasped. "Just practicing my calisthenics."

Glancing behind her, she confirmed that no one

was following her or paying much attention. The woman ahead turned down a small alley. Danielle followed her down the alley. A giant heap of razor blades spilled out of a factory door at the end of the alley. Several maintenance drones lumbered back and forth across the heap. They inhaled razor blades and spat them back out through their green hoses.

The tall woman removed a kind of block from her pocket. She pushed some buttons on it. Two of the drones approached her, wrapped their hoses under her arms, and lifted her in the air. They carried her over the heap of razor blades into the factory. The drones returned to their work, but the woman was gone.

"Maintenance drones!" Danielle said. "Do the same thing for me! Please!"

They ignored her and continued to slurp and spew razor blades. Danielle needed to find another way to get over the razor blades. She dared not step on them. If she were able to find a plank to place over the heap, she would be able to walk over it. Unfortunately, by the time she found a plank, her quarry could be anywhere.

Danielle watched the drones studiously. They were about the size and shape of stepping stools. Each one moved back and forth in its own territory. They slurped up razor blades and spat them out further away, toward the interior of the factory. Their objective was apparently to move the pile slowly into the factory. Occasionally, the drones came very close to their nearest neighbors.

When the closest drone reached the edge of the heap, Danielle stepped up on it. She remained in a low crouch and clutched the drone's sides with her hands. The drone traveled up the pile and ejected razor blades. It turned around before the next drone came close. Danielle waited patiently until the drones' cycles brought them together, and she stepped onto the next drone.

Her fingers ached from hanging on so tightly, but she could not relax. If she fell off now, she would plunge deep into the mound of razor blades. The consequences would be excruciating and possibly fatal.

When the second drone came near the third, Danielle again stepped onward. She waited a long time for the third drone to come near the fourth. For some reason, these two drones always seemed to be at least two feet apart. Danielle braced herself and leapt onto the fourth drone. Her right foot slid off the top, but she caught the round edge with her hands and steadied herself. She breathed heavily and shuddered.

The fourth drone's territory extended inside the factory. Danielle had to duck under the factory doorway every time she passed through. When the moment was right, Danielle shifted onto the fifth drone, and then the sixth, seventh, and eighth. The eighth drone worked the inner edge of the heap. Danielle jumped off the drone onto solid ground. Her legs quaked, and her breath was ragged, but she was awestruck by her own achievement.

The tall woman stood ahead.

"I was afraid you would follow me," the woman said.

"Why were you afraid?" Danielle asked.

"Because I'm always afraid."

"What are you afraid of?" Danielle asked.

"I'm afraid of the warden," the woman said.

"Join the club," Danielle said. "But why would the warden have any animosity toward you?"

"Because I'm a member of a secret guild," the woman said. "I'm in the exalted guild of technicians. We study machines and how they operate. We investigate ways to control them. We try to invent new ones. The warden monitors us closely. He lets most of us live because our inventions serve his agenda. Sometimes he gives us assignments. If we fail to complete them, we face his wrath. But mostly, he leaves us alone to exercise our creativity and ingenuity, as long as we report our discoveries to him.

"I'm not exactly forbidden to divulge our secrets because this is how we recruit new members. But the risk to new recruits is severe. Once you learn our secrets, the warden's minions will follow you forever, and you will never again find peace. You followed me here to learn from me, and I can teach you, but you must know the risk that you take."

"Somehow," Danielle said, "I suspect that I can't make my predicament any worse than it already is."

"Very well," the woman said. "Let's sit down."

The woman removed from her pocket the box with buttons. She tapped them rapidly. Two maintenance drones approached and halted. She sat down on one, and Danielle sat on the other.

"My name is Maya Spinor," she said. "I completed my first guild initiation nearly three years ago. Like all new initiates, I am compelled to master the elementary protocols in order to earn my initiation into the deeper mysteries. The elementary protocols govern the operation of this device."

Maya held up the box with buttons. There were ten buttons, labeled "0" through "9."

"This is called a transmitter," Maya continued. "It was invented by the first guildmaster; may his glory reign forever. As you've seen, I can use the transmitter to direct machines to serve my needs. I can even make them perform tasks for which they were not designed."

"I suppose that if maintenance drones had feelings, they might feel indignant about propping up our hindquarters," Danielle said.

Maya smiled. "If they feel indignant about this, how do you suppose they feel about slurping vomit and spittle on restaurant floors? I actually used to spend a lot of time worrying whether they had feelings and thoughts, which we just couldn't see. I've concluded that they have none. If it serves my needs, I do not hesitate even to destroy a machine.

"I can tell from your bravery and resourcefulness that your days are riddled with peril and matters of tremendous import. I do not know your aim, and I do not need to. Our lives are destined to intermingle only briefly. In any case, I think that the transmitter protocols will be useful, probably indispensible, to you. I can initiate you into the transmitter protocols, but you must vow never to write them down. They must be committed to memory and guarded therein."

"I promise not to write down anything you tell me," Danielle said.

"Then we can begin," Maya said. "Have you ever noticed the four-digit numbers on vehicles and drones, and above tunnel doors?"

"I think so," Danielle said. "I think they're everywhere. But I never paid any attention to them."

"Most people don't because they have no reason to," Maya said. "But actually, those are identification numbers. To control a machine, you must first type its identification number into a transmitter. According to the protocols, all identification numbers are four digits long, so there are ten thousand possible identification numbers. Clearly, there are vastly more than ten thousand vehicles, drones, and motorized doors, so each machine's identification number is not unique. When you type the identification number, you must point the transmitter at the machine. If a machine with the correct identification number is within two hundred yards of the front of the transmitter, the machine will respond. You do not need a direct line of sight. You can point the transmitter at machines on the other side of walls. The only exception is that a transmitter in one block cannot affect a machine in another block, even if you're standing on the threshold between blocks.

"There are two kinds of machines: marked and unmarked. The identification numbers of marked machines are clearly displayed on the machines. These numbers are printed on all sides of vehicles, inside and outside. If you come upon an unmarked machine, however, its number is not displayed. If you don't know the number, you can't control the machine. This is a security feature. Of course, you could use trial and error and go through all ten thousand possible numbers. To defend against this possibility, some unmarked machines will self-destruct if the wrong number is directed toward them. Usually it's nothing dangerous, just a crackle and a small puff of smoke. I've heard rumors that some machines self-destruct violently, but this topic belongs among the deeper mysteries.

"So. Suppose you know the identification number of a machine, either marked or unmarked. The simplest mode of operation is to type the machine's identification number before you type each command. If you want a machine to execute multiple commands, there is a shortcut, which I'll get to later. Each command, like each identification number, is four digits long. These are some of the most elementary commands: 7395 makes a machine move forward. 8462 makes it move backward. 4572 makes it turn left ninety degrees, and 2861 makes it turn right ninety degrees."

"Could those commands possibly be more difficult to memorize?" Danielle asked.

"I don't think so," Maya said. "The first guildmaster, may his glory reign forever, deliberately made the commands as complicated as possible. This is a precaution to discourage the unworthy."

"How many commands are there?" Danielle asked.

"Even I know many thousands, and I am but a lowly initiate," Maya said.

Danielle slapped her forehead. "Thousands of four-digit commands! Then I am among the unworthy."

"I'll only teach you a couple dozen of the most

useful commands," Maya said. "These should serve you well."

Maya taught Danielle how to make vehicles accelerate, decelerate, and halt; how to make them turn left or right through any angle; how to make them travel through the tunnels to a precinct and block of her choice; and how to open and close tunnel doors. Maya made Danielle repeat back all the numbers. Danielle needed to exert her mind strenuously, but she succeeded. She imagined each four-digit number as four dots connected to form a jagged line. The height of each dot represented the value of the corresponding digit.

"Good," Maya said. "Now, you're ready for the shortcuts. If you want a machine to execute two commands, and you don't want to type its identification number twice, then type 8302 after the identification number. Then type the two commands. If you want the machine to execute three commands, use 8303, and so on. Alternatively, if you want a single machine to execute commands indefinitely, then you type 5902 after the identification number. Type as many commands as you want. Then, to stop commanding that one machine, you type 9648. Is that clear?"

"Oh, perfectly," Danielle said.

"Here's another important fact," Maya said. "If you operate a taxi the normal way, with vocal commands, the taxi is responsible for commanding tunnel doors to open and close. If you're directing the taxi with a transmitter, you're responsible for the tunnel doors. Remember this to avoid painful collisions.

"Finally, there's one important command that's easy to remember. 4321 is the emergency shutdown command. Every machine in the entire block will freeze for about fifteen minutes. Even the ceiling lights will go off. So the entire block is plunged into darkness, unless someone has a candle burning. Now, do you have any questions?"

"Yes," Danielle said. "What happens if one person commands a machine to do one thing, but someone else commands it to do something else?"

"That's an excellent question," Maya said. "There's a hierarchy. No two transmitters occupy the same level in the hierarchy. In case of conflict, the higher transmitter wins. The only way to determine a transmitter's position in the hierarchy is to see which transmitter wins a conflict. However, it is known that the warden's transmitter is at the top of the hierarchy, of course.

"All commands except the emergency shutdown can be overridden by a higher transmitter. At the bottom of the hierarchy are vocal commands. Any other questions?"

"Just two," Danielle said. "First, are there

any surveillance machines through which the warden can see or hear what happens in distant locations?"

"To my knowledge, there are not," Maya said. "I have heard the rumor that these machines exist. The warden heard the rumor too. He wanted to make it true. He ordered some of our most exalted technicians to create these machines. They labored mightily, but so far, they have failed, and they are made to suffer greatly for their failure. I do not know if there are any ongoing efforts to invent surveillance machines. I know that there's a major guild project in the B4D block of precinct $x = -0.10$, $y = 0.37$, $z = -0.29$, but I don't think it's related to surveillance machines. I am but a lowly initiate and am not privy to the higher mysteries. What's your other question?"

"I'm searching for a secret z coordinate," Danielle said. "It's supposed to be hidden in this block. Have you seen any kind of recurring number? I think it might be fairly obvious."

Maya shook her head. "I don't know anything about that," she said. "But my grandpa always said that whenever you get stumped by some quandary, stop thinking about it and go eat a meal instead. By the end of your meal, you'll have your solution."

Danielle smiled. "Okay," she said. "I'll remember that."

"As I have stated," Maya said, "our lives are

destined to intermingle for but a short moment, and the moment is coming to an end. Here, take these two transmitters. They seem to be near the center of the hierarchy. Now, you are girded to confront your first challenge. Leave the factory without using your physical adroitness. Use a transmitter instead."

Danielle looked at the drones pacing on the heap of razor blades.

"I don't know how to control their hoses, the way you did," Danielle said.

"Oh, well, there are 274 commands for manipulating the hoses," Maya said. "The ten that are most useful are—"

"No thank you!" Danielle said. "I can't memorize any more right now! I'll make do without using the hoses."

Danielle stepped onto the drone on which she had sat. She crouched and held on with one hand. She began typing numbers into the transmitter. She felt awkward at first, but her confidence grew as the drone responded obediently. She rode the drone slowly up the heap of razor blades. The other drones moved out of the way. Danielle looked back toward Maya.

"Thank you so much for your help!" Danielle said. "I promise to find a way to repay you some day!"

Maya shook her head sadly. "You have a very good heart," Maya said. "But that is a promise you will be unable to keep."

Danielle frowned at the ominous words, but to avoid tumbling into the razor blades, she had to concentrate on her balance and her transmitter. She rode out into the alley and stepped off the drone when it halted. She walked along the alley to the street. She looked for clues. She looked for threats. She found neither.

Danielle strolled vigilantly around the entire block. There were two restaurants, four apartment buildings, three warehouses, one razor-blade factory, two tunnel doors, and 27 benches. She counted the number of words on every poster. She counted the number of people on every bench. She was unable to find any recurring numbers.

She sat on a bench with her back to a blank wall. There were no windows above her. She thought about Maya's recommendation to eat a meal when faced with a quandary. It probably was time to eat. She gagged at the thought, but her stomach was uncomfortably hollow.

A man with a frizzy, gray beard sat down next to her. Danielle scratched her chin, poising to deflect a blow.

"Be careful," the man said. "You're our only hope."

"Why are you saying this to me?" Danielle asked.

"I can lead you on the path of ascension," the man said. "It's closer than you think."

He stood and beckoned her. She followed warily. They walked for several minutes and arrived at the entrance to an alley. Danielle stopped. The alley led to a dead end.

"Behold," the man said. "The path of ascension."

"It's a dead end," Danielle said. "It leads to a concrete wall."

"A wall is no obstacle to the faithful," he said. "Faithful for me, faithful times three, faithful, you see?"

"No, I don't," Danielle said. "I don't understand."

"Understanding is of no consequence. Faith is all that matters. Come, let us ascend."

"Why don't you wait here?" Danielle said.

The man shrugged agreeably. Danielle looked back along the street. An empty taxi approached. Danielle slid her hand into her pocket and rotated the transmitter toward the taxi. She began to type commands. The taxi continued to approach, but it would halt when it arrived at the alley.

Straining all her senses, Danielle proceeded slowly down the alley. The man did not follow. At the end of the alley, Danielle examined the wall. Nothing appeared unusual. She pushed against the wall. Nothing happened.

"This is just a solid wall," Danielle shouted. "This is no path of ascension."

"That's right," the man called. "That'll teach you filthy heretic to believe whatever fool nonsense you hear."

He pulled a knife from his shirt and began running toward Danielle. She took a transmitter out of her pocket. Her fingers trembled, but she focused her mind on the commands she had learned. The taxi began accelerating down the alley toward the man. He paid no attention to it. He stared with crazed eyes at Danielle and sped toward her. The taxi slammed against his back, and he flew through the air to land on his belly. The taxi ran over his neck and screeched to a halt several paces in front of Danielle.

Danielle ran to the man. His chin rested on the wrong side of his shoulder.

"Medic!" she screamed. "Please hurry!"

She swayed frantically while she waited. A medic vehicle finally arrived and scanned the man with its red hose. It withdrew and departed.

"Come back!" Danielle shouted. "I didn't mean to kill him!"

She grabbed her head. She needed to relax. She had acted in self-defense. She saved her own life and probably the lives of other heretics. Earlier, she had accepted that she would be wounded or killed in her struggle. Now she needed to accept that she would wound and kill others. A green maintenance vehicle arrived. It extended an enormous hose and snorted up the dead man.

Danielle stepped out of the alley. She reminded herself to remain wary. She walked to a restaurant. Maybe, as Maya had suggested, she would have the solution to her quandary when she finished her meal. She entered the restaurant. Someone belched and moaned. Ahead of her in line stood a woman in a hat and a man with hairy ears. While Danielle waited, a man wearing gold lipstick came in line behind her. After him, a stooped old woman arrived, and then came three children.

When it was Danielle's turn, she placed a bowl under the dispenser and ordered, "Sweet 0.0, salty 0.1, sour 0.0, bitter 0.0, temperature 0.5." She next got her water, temperature = 0.7, and she walked reluctantly to a seat. She gathered a big scoopful of the gelatinous gruel and shoveled it into her mouth. She gagged and spat. Her lips puckered involuntarily, and her tongue twitched. She had never tasted anything so sour. It could have been sour 1.0. She took great mouthfuls of water and spat them on the floor.

A man with a waxed moustache turned toward her.

"Not from around here, are you?" he said. "Our food dispenser's a bit broken down."

"How can you stand such sourness?" Danielle groaned.

"Oh, so you got sour 1.0?" the man said. "Sometimes it's sweet 1.0. That's not so bad. Sometimes it's salty 1.0. That tends to induce immediate vomiting. Sometimes it's bitter 1.0. That usually makes people faint. Then other times, it's temperature 1.0. That's not so bad because you can see the steam and avoid the burn."

Danielle's eyes lit up. "So it always produces a 1.0 that wasn't ordered? Never 0.0? Never anything but 1.0?"

"Oh, now, it doesn't malfunction every time," the man said. "Only some of the time. But yes, when it malfunctions, it always produces an undesired 1.0. Since it just malfunctioned, it'll probably work right for a good while. Go get yourself some more."

Danielle shoved the bowl of sour slime onto the floor.

"Maintenance," she said, after the loud clatter.

She walked to the back of the line. A woman playing a kazoo stood behind the three children. Danielle kept track of the number of servings dispensed since the malfunction. The kazoo player got the sixth, and Danielle got the seventh. Danielle sat and struggled through the ordeal of eating. All the while, she continued to count servings. Because the erroneous characteristic was always 1.0, Danielle suspected that the secret z coordinate was 1.00. Her suspicion would be confirmed if the machine malfunctioned every 100 servings.

"You know what my hobby is?" said the man with the waxed moustache. "Knitting socks. Some people use the same pattern for both feet, but that doesn't makes good sense to me. The left foot is different from the right foot, so the left sock needs to have a different shape than the right sock. Now, the other unusual thing about my sock knitting is that I use only two colors of yarn. Indigo and beige. I don't like to mix them both into the same sock. It's okay if the two socks in a pair are colored differently, but I just don't like mixing colors into the same sock. That's just me.

"Now, your typical sock has all the toes all together. Well, to my way of thinking, that can get a little boring. In the same way that gloves have separate compartments for the fingers, socks can have separate compartments for the toes. But there's one thing you have to watch out for; take this from me. It's uncomfortable for a single toe to be alone in a compartment. It's okay for two toes to share a compartment, just not one by itself. The one exception to this is the big toe. The big toe can be comfortable in its own compartment.

"Now, you see, I've thought a lot about all the possible pairs of socks that I could make according to my tastes. I believe I've made a comprehensive list. Now, first, suppose both socks are indigo, and suppose all the toes are together in each sock. That's your first possibility. Next, keep the left sock the same, but in the right sock, you separate the big toe from the other four. You see the difference? Next...."

As he blathered on, Danielle pretended to be engrossed. At random intervals, she said, "Uh huh," "I see," and "Right." In fact, most of her attention remained on the food dispenser. She listened carefully to the woman who ordered the hundredth serving since the last malfunction.

"Sweet 0.2, salty 0.3, sour 0.1, bitter 0.1, temperature 0.2."

The gruel that oozed into her bowl was piping hot, clearly temperature 1.0. The woman threw the bowl on the floor and ordered again.

"...and the final combination is two beige socks with three compartments each: one for the big toe, one for the next two toes, and one for the last two toes."

"Wow," Danielle said. "That's extremely interesting."

The man smiled. "Well, if you aren't the most courteous and attentive young lady I've ever met."

He continued grinning euphorically as Danielle excused herself and walked out to the street.

"Taxi," Danielle called.

She examined the evidence in her mind. In two ways, the food dispenser seemed to encode a coordinate of 1.00. The frequency of error was one out of 100, and the erroneous characteristic was always 1.0. She felt slight uncertainty. Did a food characteristic of 1.0 encode a coordinate of 1.00, or 0.10?

Then she gasped. Information had been hidden in the rambling discourse about socks. There were five ways to parse toes into compartments so that no toe was ever alone, except possibly the big toe: put all the toes together; put the big toe by itself and keep the rest together; put the big toe and its neighbor in one compartment, and the next three in another; put the first three toes in one compartment, and the last two in another; and finally, put the big toe by itself, put the next two in a second compartment, and put the last two in a third. Each sock could have one of two colors, so there were ten possible ways to make a left sock, and ten possible ways to make a right sock. Combine each possible left sock with each possible right sock, and there were 100 possible pairs. Danielle laughed out loud. Now she was convinced that the secret coordinate was 1.00.

She stepped into the taxi feeling exhilarated. Her triumphant elation was short-lived, however, because resting on the taxi seat was Maya's head. The rest of Maya's body was nowhere to be seen.

10

Destined for the J3B block of $x = 0.38$, $y = -0.41$, and $z = 0.04$, the taxi zoomed through the blackness of the tunnels. Danielle sat silently with Maya's head and tried to understand why her own life had been spared. Was she supposed to spread her tales of horror to dissuade others from joining the search? Danielle considered the alternative explanation that Arlene had put forward. Perhaps the warden's information was incomplete. He knew that Danielle was seeking the path, and he hoped that she would uncover certain information that he lacked. Surely he had tried to find the information on his own, but perhaps at some point he reached a dead end. In this case, he could be hoping that Danielle would succeed where he had failed. If this were all true, the episodes of violence were not intended to stop Danielle altogether. The violence was intended to make her cower before the warden and surrender information upon demand.

The taxi emerged from the tunnel. A maintenance vehicle was inhaling a huge pile of oblong ping-pong balls, presumably a factory defect. Remembering her wariness, Danielle stepped out of the taxi. An occupied leisure carriage ambled past. A group of old women approached on foot. An apartment building and a library were on opposite sides of the street. There were no obvious threats. Danielle left Maya's head in the taxi because she did not know what else to do with it, and the taxi departed.

Danielle walked to the wall and leaned against it. She rubbed her stomach to help recuperate from her recent meal. One of the old women took notice.

"Stomach troubles, sweetheart?" said the woman.

Danielle nodded.

"As a little girl," the old woman said, "I discovered that my digestion improved when I ate with my eyes closed. Food is so ugly that just looking at it makes the stomach scrunch up. If you close your eyes, your stomach is much more relaxed and you feel better after you eat. I'm surprised so few people know this."

"I'll have to try that," Danielle said. "Have you really eaten with your eyes closed since you were a little girl?"

"These days, my coordination isn't so good any more, and I miss my mouth if I close both eyes. So I look in only one eye."

Danielle tensed. "What did you say?"

The old woman said, "I look with only one eye."

"That's funny," Danielle said. "I thought I heard something different. It reminded me of something I heard earlier. I was wondering if you could tell me more about it."

"I'm not the one you want to talk to, sweetheart," the old woman said. "Look for the blind woman on a bench. Follow the third street on the right."

"Thank you," Danielle said.

Danielle proceeded cautiously down the street. She hoped to avoid another false trail and fatal encounter. Up ahead, three women juggled knives. When passing the jugglers, Danielle used a transmitter to interpose a taxi between herself and them. She turned right at the third street, which was empty. After she took about fifty paces, the street turned to the left. Ahead, a young woman sat with closed eyes on a bench. Her feet were bare, and her toes wriggled in the sand surrounding the bench. Beyond the bench, the street turned again to the left. The bench faced a wall that occupied the attention of two maintenance vehicles. The first vehicle painted the wall green. The second vehicle scrubbed off the fresh green paint.

Danielle sat next to the woman.

"You sit heavily," the woman said. "You bear a weighty burden. I do not wish to shoulder it. My burden, too, is weighty."

"I'm not asking for a lot," Danielle said. "Just one number."

The woman raised her eyebrows.

"My name is Marissa Plasmid," the woman said. "Take off your shoes and rest a while. The texture of the sand is intriguing to the feet."

Danielle complied. Marissa extended her hand and lowered it onto the scarf around Danielle's wounded hand. Marissa slid her fingers under the handkerchief and over the entire scab. She began to tremble.

"The day has finally come," Marissa said. "Since antiquity, our secret has been passed from mother to first daughter. No one else has ever known. And I have doubted. I have feared. These are trying times. False prophets have arisen, and false teachings. The worst of these is the cult of the one eye. Seriously. Those people have some screws loose. Don't even set foot in the J4E block of precinct x = 0.62, y = -0.31, z = -0.74.

"But today, what has been hidden through the centuries, through the millennia, will be revealed. I had thought the secret would die with me. But now that you have come, I rejoice. We are forgiven. We are absolved. Once you learn my secret, our ascension is assured."

Marissa's neck tightened. "I spoke too soon. I was wrong. Our repentance was inadequate. Our punishment is now eternal."

"What are you talking about?" Danielle cried. "What suddenly changed?"

"Pitiless footfalls," Marissa said. "I should have known that he would follow you here. I have been so careless. I heeded so few of my mother's admonitions. This is my fault, but it reflects humanity's flaw, an ancient crime for which we can never atone."

Danielle stood and tugged Marissa's arm. "Don't just sit here and wait to be murdered! I've escaped much worse! I'll do my best to protect you!"

Marissa's arm recoiled. "I will not flee like a coward," she said. "Do not corrupt my dignity. He is much too close now. If you run, you will be struck in the back, a craven way to fall. Face your death valorously. The pain will be horrific but brief."

Danielle stomped her foot. "If you insist on martyrdom, I cannot stop you! But first tell me your secret, or else you've protected it in vain!"

"You will live but moments longer than I," Marissa said. "Whether I tell you or not, the secret perishes. Since it perishes, I know that ascension is impossible. Since ascension is impossible, I know humanity is unfit to ascend, and that is why I must not tell you my secret."

"Your logic is terrible!" Danielle said.

She squirmed in frustration. She could now hear the footsteps. She began to back away from the bench.

Marissa gasped. "The sentinel," she said.

A man appeared from around the corner. Danielle choked with rage. It was the man with the blond braid who had punched her in the stomach. She pulled a transmitter out of her pocket and aimed it at one of the maintenance vehicles.

Marissa stood and faced the man. "You have bested me," she said, "but only because all humanity is stained. You think you are better than I, but we share the same stain."

The man raised a gun and shot Marissa in the forehead. At Danielle's command, a maintenance vehicle lurched toward the man. The vehicle soon accelerated to lethal speeds, but then it shuddered to a stop. The man held a transmitter.

"What a pity that your plan has failed," the man said.

Transmitter in one hand and gun in the other, he began strolling patiently toward Danielle.

"It's been some time since anyone's come as close as you have," the man said. "It must be all the more heartbreaking to fail when the target is nearly in reach. I just may shed a tear for you. Really, I may."

He stepped over Marissa's body.

"Sometimes I just get the feeling that I'd really like to kill someone," the man said. "Do you ever get that feeling?"

"I'm starting to," Danielle said. The transmitter quaked in her hand.

The man laughed. "I'll miss that wit when you die, by my hands. Tell me, how long shall I let you struggle before I make you die?"

"Ten seconds," Danielle said.

The man frowned. "That's a surprisingly specific response. What happens then?"

"This," Danielle said, and she hurled the transmitter at the man. It smacked into his groin. He doubled over and fell choking to his knees. His eyes watered, and he fired his gun wildly. Danielle fled.

She sped around the corner. Two old men approached in a taxi. Danielle used her remaining transmitter to commandeer the vehicle. It accelerated toward her and spun screeching to a halt, facing the direction it had come from. Danielle leapt inside, and the taxi accelerated to a reckless speed before the safety belt finished slithering around her waist. The two old men clutched each other and screamed.

They zoomed past an empty leisure carriage. Up ahead was a T intersection, and just beyond that, a concrete wall. The taxi was going too fast to make the turn safely. However, it was even less safe to slow down; if the blond man saw the identification number on this taxi, he would override Danielle's commands. Danielle accelerated the taxi even more. The few pedestrians gawked from the safety of doorways.

The concrete wall was just ahead. Danielle pounded furiously at the transmitter. The taxi began screeching to the right. The tires squealed and spewed black smoke. Danielle succeeded in orienting the taxi to the right, but the taxi had too much momentum toward the wall. With a deafening shriek, the taxi skidded sideways and crashed into the wall. The left door crumpled. Danielle and the old men lurched against the safety belts but were otherwise unharmed. Thick white smoke poured from the engine.

Danielle leapt out of the taxi just as the blond man appeared at the opposite end of the road segment. He fired his gun but missed; he was quite far away. Running as fast as she could, Danielle cleared the intersection and evaded the man's line of sight, for now. She knew that he would soon find a vehicle and be close behind her.

Danielle saw an empty taxi in the road ahead. As she ran toward it, her fingers danced on the transmitter. The taxi raced backwards towards her and jerked to a halt. Danielle leapt in and rocketed down the street. The taxi ran over two maintenance drones, but the street was mercifully empty of pedestrians. Directly ahead was a door to the tunnel.

Danielle set the taxi on maximum speed and caused the tunnel door to open. She had a clear shot to the safety of the tunnel. In the darkness, the man could not follow her. Innumerable tunnel branches led to millions of precincts and billions of blocks. The man would have no idea where she went.

Danielle's hair whipped her face, and she struggled to breathe the frenzied air. Only a hundred yards remained between her and the tunnel. But then a boy stepped out of a warehouse and froze in the middle of the street. He gaped as the taxi hurtled toward him. He had never been taught to get out of the way of vehicles. Vehicles always got out of the way of people.

"Move!" Danielle screamed, but the boy was transfixed.

Cursing, Danielle pounded the buttons on the transmitter. The taxi screeched to the left, slammed its side against the wall, and spun around twice. White smoke billowed from the engine. Dizzy and choking, Danielle staggered out of the taxi. She began running towards the tunnel door.

She heard an engine roar behind her, and she knew that the blond man approached. Glancing back, she saw only the white smoke from the wreck. She heard gunfire, but the man could not see her through the smoke. She ran as fast as she could. Her chest ached, and her fingers began to feel numb. The burning in her thighs was a revelation in how severe pain could be.

The tunnel door began to lower. The man must have already known its identification number. His transmitter superseded hers in the hierarchy, so she would not be able to raise the door again. Gasping hoarsely, she tried to run even faster. She had only twenty paces to go when the bottom of the door was at the level of her neck. The door descended to the level of her waist, but she was now only ten paces away. By the time the door was knee high, she was five paces away. She slid onto her side and rolled under the door, brushing it with her shoulder. The door slammed shut behind her. She jerked to a stop. The door had closed on her hair. Without pausing to think, she jerked her head forward to tear out the hairs that were caught. Arms extended, she stumbled to the wall. Dragging one hand along the wall and extending the transmitter with the other hand, she ran onward. The scarf fell off her scarred hand, and she did not pause to retrieve it.

"Taxi!" she screamed.

In the blackness, her raspy panting sounded deafening. She was consumed with fears of plunging into an abyss, but she forced herself to run at top speed. The tunnel turned to the left and then descended sharply. She lost her balance and tumbled painfully. She maintained her grip on the transmitter. The tunnel leveled, and she stood. She found the wall and continued to run. She could now hear a vehicle approaching up ahead. From behind, light began to beam. The tunnel door was opening.

In the dimness ahead, a taxi came into view. Danielle leaped onto the seat, and a safety belt slithered around her hips. She tapped buttons on her transmitter. The taxi wheeled around with a shriek and sped off into the darkness. Gunfire sounded behind her, but she was unharmed. She had escaped. The taxi was taking her toward the B4D block of precinct $x = 0.20$, $y = -0.11$, $z = 0.07$. She had come up with this at random. No one else could know her destination. There were thousands or millions of vehicles navigating the tunnels. No one would know which vehicle was hers.

In the darkness, feeling the thrum of the engine, she panted and caught her breath. She was coated in sweat. She pushed her damp hair away from her face and leaned back. She tried to relax. She needed to think.

She halted the taxi. She sat in the darkness. It was peaceful in the tunnels. Tranquil. She would hide here forever if she did not need to eat. But she did need to eat, and besides, she was determined to continue her search for the path of ascension.

How could she return to any ordinary life of trivial diversions? The x coordinate perhaps was lost, but she had the two other coordinates: $y = 0.43$ and $z = 1.00$. There were 201 possible values for x, so there were 201 precincts with $y = 0.43$ and $z = 1.00$. Each of the 201 precincts had 100 blocks on the far plus z side, so there were still thousands of blocks that could lead to the path. Danielle needed more information.

Both Arlene and Marissa had warned her about the cult of the one eye. The people in the cult had "some screws loose." But Marissa had specified the location of the cult, and Danielle had memorized it carefully: the J4E block of precinct $x = 0.62$, $y = -0.31$, $z = -0.74$. She had been warned not to go, but she had not gotten this far by heeding warnings. Perhaps the cult had something to do with the riddle, "Look in only one eye."

She had evaded the sentinel who tried to kill her, and she had not fallen to the warden, either. She was ready to take on the cult of the one eye.

11

Danielle looked around before climbing out of the taxi. Two women sat on a bench and coughed. An emaciated man, clutching his stomach and grimacing, stepped out of a restaurant. A maintenance vehicle slurped a lone shoe off the street. This block appeared to be typical. Danielle got out of the taxi and went into a warehouse to find a pair of gloves to conceal the scar on her hand.

Danielle left the warehouse and walked down the street. She did not know how to find a cult. Could she just ask someone? Would that alert unfriendly elements? Then she paused. A single eye was carved into a door just past a warehouse. She pushed against the door, and it opened. Several pedestrians strolled the street, but none paid her any attention.

The door opened to a long corridor with doors on either side. Danielle proceeded warily down the corridor. Some of the doors were open and led to small libraries. A few people sat reading at tables. No one looked up when Danielle passed by.

The last door on the left had an eye carved on it. Danielle pushed the door. It swung open to an empty hall with no other doors. A dead end. Apprehensive, Danielle walked down the hall. At the end of the hall, she pushed the wall, but nothing happened. Frustrated, she looked around. The wall panels were white and held up by matching white screws. Then Danielle remembered the warning about the cult: they have some screws loose. She dragged her hand along the wall and found one panel whose screws jutted out. She was able to turn them with her fingers. She removed the screws and lifted the panel. Beyond was a short hallway with a door on the left side. She stepped into the hallway and repositioned the panel as well as she could. She walked to the door.

The door was open and led to a room with a circle of seven cushions in the far corner. Two people sat on adjacent cushions. One was a man with straight black hair. His eyes were closed, and he rubbed his head with his hands. To his right sat a woman with a smooth face but many gray hairs. She smiled warmly at Danielle. Danielle noticed that the woman's hands rested on two bricks.

"Welcome!" the woman said. "Come sit down!"

With trepidation, Danielle approached her. There were no other doors to this room, and there were no windows. Without any machines around, Danielle's transmitter was useless, and she had no other defense. Danielle sat cautiously beside the woman. Danielle kept a close eye on the bricks.

"My name's Stephanie Biome," the woman said. "What's yours?"

"Amanda Ligand," Danielle said. She did not know why she lied.

"Is this your first time?" Stephanie asked.

"Well, yes," Danielle said.

"You don't need to be nervous," Stephanie said. Her smile was very warm. "We have a great seer. He has a lot of experience helping newcomers. You'll purge even more sins than you expect."

"Oh," Danielle said. "Wow. That sounds great."

Stephanie laughed. She spoke joyfully. "You're going to feel so much better when you've purged your sins. I just love being here when there's a newcomer."

"I—I'm sorry to betray my ignorance," Danielle said, "but what are the bricks for?"

"Oh," Stephanie said. "They're for my offering. I've put a lot of thought into my offering this time. What are you doing for your offering?"

"Oh," Danielle said. "I thought I'd just decide when the time comes."

Stephanie beamed. "That's a good idea. I often do that as well. Maybe the seer will say something to inspire you."

"Can you tell me more about your seer?" Danielle asked.

"I'd love to," Stephanie giggled. "He's very wise. He's been to the opening of the path, but his sins had not all been purged. That's why horrendous things happened to him there. If you approach the opening to the path, you must be thoroughly cleansed. Otherwise, your punishments will be excruciating. Usually, if this happens to you, you give up on ascension. You never want to return to the opening of the path. But our seer did not give up! He continues to purge his sins so that one day he may try again!"

"The opening of the path...of ascension?" Danielle said.

"Yes," Stephanie said. "Maybe, when our sins are all purged, we can go there together."

"You know where the opening of the path is?" Danielle said.

"Of course," Stephanie said. "Everyone does. It's too big to fit in one block, so there are four, all in precinct x = 0.00, y = 0.00, z = 1.00. The opening of the path occupies the central top blocks: E4J, F4J, E5J, and F5J. It thrills me to think about it! Someday I'll be ready! But first, I must purge my many sins so that I will not face gruesome punishment."

"That seems wise," Danielle said.

A bald man carrying a hammer entered the room and sat down on the other side of Danielle. She felt that she was in terrible danger. She was certain that she needed to leave at once, but she did not know how to do so peacefully.

"Stephanie," Danielle said, "can you tell me where the nearest bathroom is? I'll be right back."

Stephanie squealed in delight. "You don't really have to go," she said. "This happens to all newcomers. The sinful flesh clings desperately to its sins. It does not want you to purge sin, for it is made of sin. So it tries to lure you away just before your sins are purged. Don't worry. You'll forget all about going to the bathroom once we start purging our sins."

Danielle's palms sweated fiercely within her gloves. Her mind plunged into panic, and she strained to keep her voice calm.

"Stephanie," Danielle said, "I really think I may be a rare exception here. I'm sure I really have to go."

"Of course not!" Stephanie laughed. "You'll see! How funny this will seem after we've purged sins together! We will laugh about this often.

And besides, the seer has come! Look at me, I'm trembling in anticipation of purging my sins!"

But Danielle did not look at her; Danielle looked to the door. A man with long white hair crept in on his belly. He wore an eye patch, and he had no feet. He dragged himself forward with his hands. A metal bowl containing a metal mallet rested on his back. He was followed by an enormously muscular man, clearly an athlete of some sort. The muscular man held a thick metal pole. He entered the room and closed the door. He glowered at Danielle.

"I'm really glad you came," Stephanie whispered, patting Danielle's knee. "You're never going to forget this."

The seer crept over to the circle of cushions. He removed the bowl from his back and placed it in the center of the circle. He climbed onto the cushion to the left of the man with black hair. Danielle was frantic with terror, but she tried to appear calm.

"What loathsome sinners we are!" the seer roared. "What vile degenerates! How unworthy we are of clemency! How unworthy we are of redemption! How suitable it is to be trapped in these corrupt fleshly bodies, these sacks of filth! If you want to be as revolted by your sins as heaven is, just look in the toilet after you sit upon it! Take a close look! Take a deep breath! That is what you are made of! That is just a small sample of your putrescence, oozing out! That is the nature of your sins, made visible for you to see!

"How laughable it is for us to seek ascension! How pitiful! How futile must be our efforts! And yet, heaven's mercy is so abundant that we have cause for hope! If our repentance is sincere and all our sins are purged, then we may yet aspire to the opening of the path! We must not falter in our efforts! We must not be dissuaded! We must be diligent in the purging of our sins!

"How joyous it is to purge our sins! How jubilant the feeling! And yet our corrupt fleshly bodies protest violently! They will try to convince you that your ecstasy is pain! You must muster all your will to resist this false message! Do not be afraid! I am here to guide you through it! We will each purge our sins today, and I will be the first!"

He seized the metal mallet from the bowl and pressed his other hand against the floor. He raised the mallet and slammed it against his thumbnail. His eyelids flickered, and he shuddered briefly. He tore off a bloody sliver of his thumbnail and dropped it in the bowl. He slid the bowl to the man with black hair. Danielle glanced at the man guarding the door. He continued to glare at her. Danielle fought down nausea.

The man with black hair took a fistful of his own hair and tore it out. The ripping was audible. He screamed, and the veins bulged in his head.

"You have purged many sins," said the seer.

The man with black hair dropped the fistful of hair into the bowl and slid it to Stephanie.

Stephanie caressed the bricks.

"I have thought a lot about my offering today," Stephanie said, addressing the seer. "You have taught us well that fleshly pleasures only anchor us to these corrupt, decaying bodies. Fleshly pleasures are not only sinful; they make us cling to our sins instead of purging them. You have taught us to harness our misguided attachment to fleshly pleasure! You have taught us to harness our misguided fear of fleshly pain! The corrupt thrill of fleshly pleasure becomes the true thrill of purging sins! The corrupt fear of fleshly pain becomes the true fear of retaining our sins!

"May the false pain I soon suffer remind me of the true pain of retaining sin," Stephanie said. She lifted the bricks, raising one high above her head.

Danielle looked away. Her heart pounded in her throat. She heard a swift inhalation, a sickening smack, and a scream so high-pitched that it sounded like a whistle. Danielle turned back to Stephanie. Stephanie's head hung backward, and her eyes were wide with horror. She dropped the bricks and clawed the air with quaking fingers. She gasped hoarsely and uttered a series of deep, raspy bellows. When she stopped shaking, she squeezed a thick drop of blood from her tongue into the metal bowl.

"A most suitable offering," said the seer.

Stephanie slid the bowl to Danielle. Danielle's vision began to dim, and she had to remind herself to breathe. She drew a deep breath, shaking fiercely. She spoke in a quavering voice.

"This is my first time, and I know I have accumulated many sins," Danielle said. "Earlier today, I was delirious with the joyful anticipation of purging my sins for the first time! I was so excited, so thrilled to finally begin purging my sins, that I just couldn't wait. I purged my sins before I even came here. I can show you; it's on my hand."

"You surely did not purge all your sins," the seer said, "and it is better when others witness it to be similarly inspired. Come, purge some more now, and you'll feel even better."

"I thought—I thought that since this was my first time," Danielle said, "I should go slow, lest in my ecstasy of purging sins, I aspire too soon to the opening of the path."

"Nonsense!" the seer said. "You expose your ignorance with every word! I can tell that you are a very grave sinner. But if you must, show us your hand, and we shall see how we must proceed."

With unsteady fingers, Danielle removed her left glove. Her scabs outlined the shape of one eye.

"Blasphemy!" the seer screamed.

"Blasphemy!" repeated Stephanie, the black-haired man, and the bald man.

"You did not purge any sins with your blasphemy!" the seer raged. "You only magnified them! Since you clearly do not know how to purge your sins, we will purge them for you!"

Danielle took one of the bricks and bashed it against the bald man's head. He crumpled. Danielle turned and thrust the brick at Stephanie's head. Stephanie tried to dodge, but the corner of the brick caught her in the temple. The impact made a cracking sound, and Stephanie fell. The man with black hair reached for the other brick, but Danielle struck him down before he could lift it.

Brandishing his thick pole, the door guard ran toward Danielle, but she seized the bald man's hammer and raised it over the seer's head.

Danielle cried to the seer, "Tell him to back off or I will kill you, and I don't care if I die next!"

"Jimmy, back away," the seer said mildly.

"Tell him to drop the pole near the door."

"Do as she says, Jimmy."

"Jimmy, be a good fellow," Danielle said, "and let's slowly trade places. Your beloved leader and I will move clockwise to the door, and you will move clockwise to the cushions. You will stay as far from us as possible at all times."

The men obeyed. Danielle picked up the metal pole.

"Jimmy, my good man," Danielle said, "you'll just stay where you are while the seer escorts me out to the street. If I catch one glimpse of you in the hallway, I'll crush the seer's skull."

Danielle and the seer proceeded down the hallway to the removable panel. Danielle pushed the panel, but it did not budge.

"Did someone screw it in from the other side?" Danielle asked.

The seer nodded.

"I think you'll live a lot longer if you find a way to remove this obstacle," Danielle said.

"Brenda!" the seer called. "Remove the panel!"

"Oh, and Brenda," Danielle shouted, "I'm holding a good, solid hammer that's desperate to crack open your seer's hoary head. I'm exerting all my strength to restrain the hammer, so I'd better not be distracted when the panel comes down. You'd better be alone and unarmed."

A soft grinding sound came from the other side of the panel. Danielle adjusted her grip on the hammer and the pole.

"I suppose I should congratulate you on being the most execrable person I've ever met," Danielle said to the seer. "Tell me, were you born this way, or did you have to work up to it?"

"Fine words, coming from a violent intruder!" the seer exclaimed. "I never laid a finger on any of my flock! I think you killed Stephanie. She has thin bones. Bob and Jeffrey will soon be dead if they don't get to a medic, and you seem to have no interest in saving their lives! You'd rather pursue your own savagery!"

"I acted in self defense!" Danielle snapped.

"Self defense?" the seer laughed incredulously. "Did anyone make the slightest move to harm you before you struck down your first two victims?"

"Well, no, but Jimmy and the black-haired guy tried to attack me."

"That's because you'd just brutalized two people! Jimmy and Sam were the ones acting in self defense, not you!"

"Enough of your poison words!" Danielle said. "You told them to purge my sins, which clearly would have involved horrific violence against me."

"You just tell yourself that, if it makes you feel less guilty," the seer said. "You don't know what we were going to do. Your deeply flawed assumption cost three people their lives."

"It's about to be four, if you don't shut your mouth!" Danielle said.

"What shall I tell Stephanie's mother? What shall I tell her five-year-old son?"

"Stop it! Stop it!" Danielle cried. "I'm not as weak-willed as your pitiful flock! I know I did the right thing!"

"Feel the weight of your crimes," the seer said. "Feel the depth of your shame. As gravely as you have sinned, you need not despair. You can always decide to purge your sins."

"I'm not listening to you anymore!" Danielle said.

"Think of the sobs of Stephanie's son," the seer said. "Think of the wails of her mother. This is the work of your hands. How can you bear to keep this guilt inside you? I can help you release it."

Tears were streaming down Danielle's cheeks when the panel clattered to the ground. Brenda stood aside as Danielle and the seer advanced toward the street. Danielle called a taxi and a leisure carriage. She instructed the seer to wait just inside the door to the street. She went outside and made the leisure carriage crash into the door, blocking it.

She sat in the taxi and proceeded toward the tunnel door. A formation of cymbal players blocked her way.

"Move, move, move! Out of the way!" Danielle shouted.

The formation parted slowly in front of the taxi and reformed right behind it. Cymbal players surrounded the taxi. Danielle was forced to ride very slowly, but she told herself she was safe; the cult of the one eye was sealed in its building until a maintenance vehicle cleared the wrecked carriage.

Up ahead, Jimmy appeared, thumping the metal mallet against his palm. He must have left the building through another door. Jimmy spotted Danielle and barreled toward her. The cymbal players scrambled to get out of his way. When a clear path opened between Jimmy and the taxi, the taxi sped forward, knocking him down. The speed had been insufficient to kill him, and Danielle had to run him over three times before he stopped screaming.

After entering the tunnel, Danielle had a sudden insight: Stephanie had been like a leisure carriage whose cartridge was deliberately put in upside down.

12

The journey through the tunnels seemed interminable. Danielle traveled toward one of the top central blocks of the $x = 0.00$, $y = 0.00$, $z = 1.00$ precinct. There, according to Stephanie's testimony, the opening of the path would be found. Stephanie had feared that she would suffer gruesome punishment if she prematurely approached the opening of the path. For this reason, Danielle was reluctant to go, but she had no other leads. She shoved the head of her hammer as deeply as possible in her pocket, and she gripped the metal pole with both hands. She was ready for trouble. Unfortunately, she felt trouble brewing in her lower intestines. She would need a bathroom soon.

The taxi emerged to a horrifying scene. A maintenance drone was attempting to slurp up a dead baby, but the green hose was too small.

"Maintenance vehicle," Danielle said.

She got out of the taxi and began walking down the street. A man approached. He had hooks for hands. Danielle halted and raised her pole defensively.

"Three different letters, three different numbers," the man said.

"That's a new one," Danielle said. "What's that supposed to mean?"

"You just let me do my job, and I'll let you do yours," he said.

"Can you at least tell me where the nearest bathroom is?" Danielle said.

"It's in the restaurant," he said. "Third building on the right. Oh, and you might want to switch your glove to your other hand."

"Oh! Thank you!" Danielle said.

She had taken off one glove to reveal her wounded hand to the cult. Her blasphemous wound was still exposed. How had she become so careless? She switched her glove from her right hand to her left.

"I hope your kindness to me does not endanger you," Danielle said.

"You may think that I am helping you," the man said, "but I am actually helping myself. It is an ancient law that if you risk your life for someone in need, then you merit the highest reward, in this life or the next."

Danielle watched the man disappear into a building. She paused in wonderment. She seemed to have as many unexpected allies as enemies. This made her efforts all the more important. She must not disappoint those who struggled and sacrificed to support her.

Outside the door to the restaurant, two maintenance drones circled each other, extending their hoses menacingly. Danielle walked into the restaurant and choked on the familiar odor of food. Two women and one man occupied the restaurant; all three of them had thinning hair. Danielle walked to the back wall, but the three people rose to gather in front of the bathroom door.

"Excuse me," Danielle said. "I think I should be first to use the bathroom. I started walking here first."

"We're not here to use it," the man said.

"We're here to listen outside the door," one of the women said.

"Just get out of my way!" Danielle said, swinging her pole.

Danielle kicked open the door and confirmed that the bathroom was unoccupied. She backed in, glared at the three spectators, and slammed the door. She heard their wet, raspy breathing through the door. They cheered and hooted after each explosive release.

Danielle burst out of the bathroom, jabbing the pole in the air.

"The next performance is in four hours," she snarled. "Don't miss it."

The man furrowed his brow. "What kind of performance?"

"Just get out of my way!" Danielle said again.

As she strode out of the restaurant, she heard one of the women say, "Do Charles and Nate know?"

"Charles and Nate are coming," the man said.

Danielle walked out onto the street. She circumvented the two circling drones and confronted two men who approached. One man wore a tuxedo and top hat. The other man was the fattest person Danielle had ever seen. His belly bulged out from under his shirt.

"Greetings, and welcome!" called the man in the tuxedo. He smiled broadly and twiddled his fingers along the edge of his hat. "Tell me, please, are you a heretic?"

Danielle shifted the pole in her hands, seeking the optimal grip for a lethal attack.

"No," Danielle said. "I denounce all heresy. Heretics slander the memory of our illustrious forebears."

The man smiled sadly.

"It is my grim duty to confound you with the fact that only heretics have ever heard of heresy," he said.

"By that logic, you're a heretic," Danielle said. She glanced around. The three people in the restaurant peered intently from the doorway. The fat man began to drool. The two drones continued to circle each other.

"Nate does not care much for logic," said the man in the tuxedo. "It hurts his poor head. It makes his poor tummy rumble. Isn't that right, Nate?"

"Nate is hungry," the fat man said. He took a lumbering step toward Danielle.

"Taxi," Danielle said.

"Cancel taxi request," sighed the man in the tuxedo.

Danielle whirled the pole into Nate's head. Her wrists ached from the shock of the impact.

"Nate doesn't like getting hit in the head," Nate said.

Gasping, Danielle dropped the pole and pulled the hammer from her pocket. Aiming for Nate's eye, she swung the hammer with all her might. Nate blocked the blow with his elbow.

"Nate doesn't like getting hit in the elbow," Nate said.

Nate slammed his fist into Danielle's ribs. She recoiled and landed on her back. The hammer skittered across the street and into the hose of a maintenance drone. Crushing pains ripped through Danielle's side. She felt as though a taxi were parked on her ribcage. Every attempt to inhale intensified her suffering. She forced herself to take small sips of air, though each sip seemed to slash through some soft, vital organ. Nate lumbered toward her.

"Take the feet first so the rest can't run away," said the man in the tuxedo.

"Nate wants to start with the tender morsels," Nate said. "Nate wants to start with the lips."

"Very well," sighed the man in the top hat. "It's too damaged to run away, anyway."

"Orange vapor," Danielle whispered.

The caustic vapor jetted from tiny holes in the street.

"Vapor off," the man in the top hat said irritably.

The tiny holes in the street began to close. Danielle turned her head and sucked orange vapor into her mouth. Her eyes bulged at the searing pain in her tongue and gums. She wondered if her tongue and gums were disintegrating and bleeding. She almost forgot the pain in her side. Her chest ached for breath, but she somehow waited until Nate squatted beside her and lowered his slavering face near her mouth. She forcefully blew the orange vapor into his eye. The effort sent shocking spasms through her side. Nate fell back on his haunches.

"Nate doesn't like being blinded," Nate said,

blinking fiercely and rubbing his eyes.

"It only got your left eye," said the man in the tuxedo. "Cover your left eye with your hand."

Nate covered his right eye as his left eye watered and swelled.

"That's not your left eye!" shouted the man in the tuxedo. "Cover your other eye!"

Nate raised his other hand and now had both eyes covered.

"Now uncover the first eye! Good. That's better, isn't it?"

Danielle coughed as stinging pains spread down her throat, and she winced at the pangs in her side. She heard the thrum of a vehicle. She rolled her head to see a taxi approaching. She read the identification number. She reached a quaking arm into her pocket to find the transmitter. Now she had a real chance to survive. Then her heart sank. The man stepping out of the taxi had a blond braid. It was the man who had killed Marissa. He, at least, had executed her cleanly. Maybe he would take pity on Danielle.

"Please," Danielle croaked. "Help."

The blond man smiled cruelly. "It doesn't appear that they need any help," he said. "They're doing an admirable job on their own."

Danielle whimpered.

"Welcome! Greetings!" said the man in the tuxedo. "Tell me please, are you a heretic?"

The blond man sneered. "I'm the one who kills heretics."

"Why, that's the very worst kind of heretic!" said the man in the tuxedo.

"And the tastiest," said Nate, aiming his good eye at the blond man.

"Leave the punched one," said the man in the tuxedo. "It's too damaged to run away. Take the new one. Take the feet first so the rest can't run away."

Nate lurched to his feet. He held his left eye and lumbered toward the blond man, who raised his gun.

"I do not wish to kill you," the blond man said. "You kill heretics, and I kill heretics. It serves my purpose to let you live. Of course, I'll kill you if I have to."

Nate continued to approach the blond man. The blond man sighed and shot Nate in the ear.

"Nate doesn't like getting shot in the ear," Nate said.

Alarm flickered across the blond man's face, and he pulled the trigger again. This time, nothing happened. Nate slammed his fist into the blond man's mouth. The blond man landed on his back. The gun spun along the street, and a maintenance drone slurped it up. The blond man spat blood and teeth, and he pulled a transmitter from his pocket. Nate stepped on the transmitter, crushing it. Nate seized the blond man's ankle and threw off his boot. The blond man kicked and squirmed but could not escape.

Danielle aimed her transmitter at the taxi. It screeched towards her and spun around to face the tunnel at the end of the street. Grimacing at the pain in her side, she hoisted herself into the taxi and sped away. She heard a crunch and a scream, and she looked back. Nate had just bitten off the blond man's toe. Danielle winced.

"I can't believe I'm doing this," she said to herself, "but I was just told that you if you risk your life for someone in need, then you merit the highest reward."

She wheeled the taxi around and sent it hurtling at full speed into Nate. He soared through the air and landed on his belly.

"Nate doesn't like getting hit by a taxi," Nate said, slowly rising to his knees.

The man in the tuxedo fled into a building.

"Get in!" Danielle screamed at the blond man. "Hurry! That fat cannibal is indestructible!"

Danielle gripped the man's elbows and pulled hard. He groaned and clambered onto the seat. The taxi sped again toward the tunnel door.

The man spat weakly, and thick blood hung from his lips. "The tunnel door's identification number is 4972. It's unmarked."

"Oh! Thank you!" Danielle said.

She raised the tunnel door, and the taxi whisked them into darkness.

13

"First of all," the man gurgled in the blackness, "thank you. I can't tell you how much it means to me that you saved my life. And it's not just that I have a particular fondness for my own life. It's the way you saved me. You risked your own life to save someone who tried to kill you and who showed you nothing but cruelty. I have never before witnessed such selfless courage and compassion. I had not known that humanity was capable of such virtue."

"Well, don't give me too much credit," Danielle said, swallowing painfully. Her throat was swollen from contact with the orange vapor. "I'm starting to lose track of how many people I killed today. Maybe I'm just trying to redeem myself. And before you bleed to death and spoil my redemption, let's get you a medic."

Danielle halted the taxi and called a medic. The man muttered something that Danielle could not understand. She asked him to repeat it.

"Please, no tattoos," he said.

Danielle began to laugh, but then she yelped at the ache in her side.

"Okay," Danielle said, "on the condition that you don't make me laugh. My ribs are bruised."

"It's a deal," the man said. "Well, the least I owe you is an introduction. My name's Roger Clade, and I'm very sorry I inconvenienced you in various ways, such as by trying to kill you."

"You inconvenienced me pretty successfully when you killed the only person who knew an invaluable secret," Danielle said.

"I told you I was sorry!" Roger said. "Please don't rub it in! Maybe I, too, can redeem myself for the murders I committed. I don't want to kill you anymore. I don't even want to thwart your efforts. In fact, I want to help you. I'm good at solving problems. But you'll have to trust me enough to tell me everything you've learned."

"Give me one good reason I should trust you," Danielle said.

"I will," Roger said, "in a minute. I hear the medic approaching."

Danielle heard some whirring noises and a groan.

After a few minutes, Roger said, "I'm good as new. I've got a nice prosthetic toe and several false teeth. My mouth's all numb. I'll be drooling for a while. Do you need the medic?"

"No," Danielle said. "I think I'm recovering on my own. So go on, why should I trust you?"

"I'd hid an extra gun under the taxi seat," Roger said. "Here, take it. Please don't pull the trigger. The gun's pointing at me."

Incredulous, Danielle took the gun.

"I'll shoot a hole through the roof of the taxi to make sure this is a real gun," Danielle said. "So cover your ears if you want to."

"I'm used to the sound. I'll cover your ears, if you'd like."

"Oh! Well, I think I would like that, very much," Danielle said. "That's so—what do the troubadours say?—chivalrous of you."

Roger pressed his palms against Danielle's ears, and she shot a hole through the roof. Roger withdrew, and Danielle reached up to confirm that the roof was now perforated.

"I'm not sure I want the gun," she said. "If I put it in my pocket, might it accidentally fire?"

"That's rare, but it does happen," the man said. "One time I shattered my thigh bone that way. A medic fixed me up pretty good. My limp is imperceptible as long as the temperature is at least 0.4."

"Here. You can have the gun back," Danielle said. "You've won my trust. Just please don't pull the trigger. It's again pointing at you."

Roger chuckled. "Thanks. I know a place where we'll be safe. We can rest and plan our next step. May I direct the taxi?"

Danielle shrugged. "You might as well," she said.

The taxi rumbled onward through the darkness, and Danielle marveled at her strange new alliance.

14

The taxi dropped them off in a block unlike any Danielle had ever seen. Small, identical buildings lined the street. A combination padlock hung from each door. Danielle followed Roger to one of the buildings. She wondered if he knew that she memorized the combination as he dialed it.

"What is this place?" Danielle asked.

"These are the barracks of the guardians of the path, secret warriors sworn to protect heaven by keeping people out," Roger said. "Our oath is normally interpreted as a mandate to kill anyone in search of the path. One of the more extreme interpretations is that we must kill anyone with any knowledge of the path. But don't worry, I've broken my oath. The oath is based on the assumption that no people are worthy to enter heaven. However, I have witnessed your unique worthiness in your selfless valor and kind-hearted magnanimity."

"What about the rest of the guardians?" Danielle asked. "Are they still sworn to kill me?"

"I'm the last of the guardians," Roger said. "And since I'm the last guardian, I have a special title: I'm known as the sentinel. That's not from any ancient ballad or anything. I chose that sobriquet just because I like it. It suits me, don't you think?"

"Oh yes, it's simply dashing," Danielle said. "What happened to the rest of the guardians?"

"I killed them," Roger said. "I was afraid they were double agents for the warden. When I set my mind to something, I do it all the way. And now, I've set my mind to serving you, so you can relax."

"I'm a little unnerved by your penchant for homicide," Danielle said, "but I'll just hope your loyalties don't shift again."

"They won't," Roger said. "Everything has changed, now that I've met someone worthy of heaven."

Roger opened the door to the building. A large room contained a bed, a table, several cushioned chairs, two padlocked chests, and a food dispenser. A side door led to a bathroom.

"I've never seen an apartment with its own

food dispenser," Danielle said.

"Membership in a secret warrior caste has its perks," Roger said. "Have a seat. These are the most comfortable chairs I've ever found. I think you could really use a rest. You're wheezing and groaning with each breath."

"Oh, sorry," Danielle said, lowering herself gingerly into a chair. Roger sat across from her.

"If you're so suspicious of the warden," Danielle said, "why didn't you band with the other guardians to fight him? Now that you're alone, aren't you less powerful?"

Roger shrugged. "There was an uneasy truce between the guardians and the warden. The warden wanted to find the path of ascension, but he didn't want anyone to beat him to it, so he killed most of the path seekers. He didn't want too many seekers to keep track of. He spared the seekers who seemed the most promising, but he left them terrorized so that they would yield up their secrets upon capture. So the warden and the guardians shared the goal of imperiling the path seekers. With limited resources, we needed the warden's assistance, and he needed ours."

"I think I can understand the motivation to become a guardian," Danielle said. "Just looking around at our pettiness, our irritability, our heartlessness and selfishness, can easily convince you that we would only wreak havoc if admitted to a perfect world. But why would anyone work for the warden? What can the warden give people that they don't already have? And even the warden himself, what is his motivation? Why would anyone want to be warden?"

"The warden knows that if he doesn't seize power, then someone else will," Roger said. "He must be master to avoid being slave. And as for his minions, he finds various ways to reward their services. He can offer information. Guns. Better food."

"For better food, even I would work for the warden," Danielle said.

"I don't think it's truly better," Roger laughed. "Only the presentation is better. Finer crockery. Perfumed candles."

"Wait a minute," Danielle said. "How do you know so much about the warden?"

"I used to work for him," Roger said. "But relax! I know what you're thinking. You're thinking that my loyalties shift at the slightest provocation, which means you have no assurance that I'll remain loyal to you. But really, it takes a lot to shift my loyalties. Whatever I do, I do all the way, and it's hard to turn me around. I stopped working for the warden only because he discharged me from his retinue. It wasn't my choice."

"Why were you discharged?" Danielle said.

"It was a trivial matter," Roger said. "The warden asked me to paint a portrait of him. I'm highly regarded for my portraiture. Have you ever been to the portrait gallery in the I5D block of precinct x = 0.06, y = -0.14, z = 0.22? No? Well, I have a large collection there. Anyway, I painted the warden's portrait, and he didn't like it."

"Why didn't he like it?" Danielle asked.

"It looked just like him," Roger said.

Danielle laughed.

"You're lucky he did no worse than discharge you," she said. "You're lucky he didn't kill you."

"I suppose I am," Roger said. "The warden has a soft spot for me in his icy heart. I earned that soft spot. Years earlier, I defended his favorite mistress, Kristin Xylem. It happened while I was painting her portrait. Actually, this was how I first met the warden.

"I had been an ordinary man with ordinary hobbies, like painting, especially portraiture. I was known for completing highly lifelike and detailed portraits within an hour. The warden—I didn't yet know he was the warden—heard my reputation and asked me to paint a portrait of his favorite mistress. That's actually the expression he used: favorite mistress. I should have known there was something unsavory about him.

"So I agreed to paint the portrait. Kristin sat in front of a cascading fountain. She was draped in a white sheet. After an hour, the portrait was nearly finished. Kristin had been admirably cooperative. She held herself almost perfectly still. She even asked for permission to scratch an itch on her shoulder. All I had left to do was find the perfect color for her eyes. I kept thinking I mixed the right color on my palette, but every time I painted it onto the canvass, I saw that it wasn't correct. The incorrect colors accumulated on the canvas, creating a three-dimensional effect that was unintentional but not unsuitable.

"Then a shaggy brute walked out of the crowd and said, 'I know how to improve the portrait!' and he tried to pull off Kristen's sheet. She pulled back, but the brute was much stronger than she, and she was about to lose the battle. So I shouted out, 'Excuse me sir, would you mind having some respect for the lady!'

"With a look of pure contempt in his eye, he strutted over to me and punched me in the face, which, come to think of it, is emerging as a recurrent theme in my life. I landed on my back but somehow managed to retain my grip on my paintbrush and palette. The brute kneeled on my stomach and prepared to batter my face, when I dabbed paint onto each of his eyeballs. He screamed for a medic and staggered blindly away, and I completed the portrait. The brute's tears combined with the paint on the brush to form exactly the color I needed.

"The next day, the warden thanked me for the portrait and for defending his favorite mistress. He informed me that the medic had been unable to save the brute's eyesight. I had blinded the brute for life. The warden asked me how I felt about that. I said, 'I'm grateful that he won't be able to ogle your favorite mistress anymore,' and the warden replied, 'That's exactly the sort of remorselessness I've been looking for.'

"He explained that he was dedicated to the common good. The peaceful pursuit of leisure, envisioned by our forebears, was threatened by inflammatory rumors. What would happen if people were convinced that the food dispensers were breaking down? There would be frantic mobs jammed into restaurants. People would hoard what they could and steal what others hoarded. The descent into violent chaos would be rapid and irreversible. To preserve the common good, we needed to squelch the inflammatory rumors and their reckless disseminators.

"I believed him. He gave me a gun and a transmitter and taught me how to use them. I carried out surveillance and executions as he instructed me. I called him 'Wardy.' We all did, who worked for him. Behind his back, we referred to him as 'the baby' because he has no hair, and he has no teeth. We joked that he played with rattles and drank from a bottle.

"I learned so much. I studied with the technicians. I even learned some of their higher mysteries, such as the doctrine that our last names hide ancient secrets. I was happy. I had always believed that portraiture, while an admirable pastime, was not my true calling. I thought that I had found my calling in the warden's service. When he discharged me, I lost more than a source of fine crockery. I lost my purpose in life.

"I fell into a kind of depression. I breathed too much white vapor. I spent too much time in leisure carriages, alone. I didn't eat enough. I didn't drink enough. Once I didn't drink anything for almost three days. I lay near death. My heartbeats rang in my ears with a tinny timbre, like dented chimes. I vomited in my bed and didn't rise to clean it.

"My breaths came in labored gasps, and I disavowed the effort to continue breathing. I lay motionless and waited for my thoughts, too, to cease. Then I was overcome by violent shaking, and I beheld the most otherworldly visions: towering columns, swaying and intricately textured, sinuously branching, and crowned with the most breathtaking green mosaic. Each mosaic tile was soft and fluttery and shifting constantly, creating a kaleidoscope of never-ending freshness and delight.

"I beheld the entire life cycle of these enchanted beings! They began as tiny pebbles buried in the ground. There, packed in the blackness, in the moistness, embraced in a womb of infinite size, they began to grow. They ascended upward, spiraling, creeping, so slowly, so gently. They expanded and flourished, reaching upward, stretching outward, burrowing into the ground with innumerable feet as they caress the air with innumerable hands. From their fingertips, every year they produced countless new pebbles, which cascaded to the ground to begin the cycle anew.

"I knew that I beheld the archangels of heaven, and I knew that I was consecrated to defend them. For I saw that the angels, though much smaller than the archangels, had their own defenses: piercing teeth, slashing fingernails, sharp protrusions, and crippling poisons. However, the archangels, for defense, had only me. So I vowed to be vigilant. I vowed to secure the passage to heaven by obscuring it forever.

"I was remorseless in my pursuit and destruction of heaven seekers. Sometimes, following the warden's example, I spared the lives of seekers so that they would spread their tales of horror. And it's not that I loathe humanity. I love humanity as much as anyone else does. It's just that I love the archangels so much more. I need to shield them from humanity's deadly avarice. But you are not avaricious. You have demonstrated the purity of your heart, so I will escort you to heaven, if that is what you wish."

"I gladly accept your assistance," Danielle said, "but unless you know something I don't, our information is incomplete. I have only two of the path's coordinates, and you killed the last person who knew the third."

"I said I was sorry!" Roger said. "Please stop bringing that up! I'll make it up to you. Tell me what you know, and I'll figure out the rest."

"Okay," Danielle said. "Okay. We'll try that. But first I need to sleep. In the past two days, I've had my hand slashed; my cheek and elbow bruised; and my mouth, stomach, and ribs punched. And I'm probably forgetting something. By the way, I'm sorry I flung that transmitter at you, but I saw no other choice."

"Right in the groin!" Roger said. "So dastardly!"

"I was aiming for your head," Danielle said.

They laughed.

"Before you sleep, would you like some food?" Roger offered. "I can demonstrate the salubrious influence of fine crockery."

Danielle laughed. "Very well. We shall see whether I salute this salubrious influence."

"And if it leads to salivation, then, surely, that's salvation," Roger said.

He took several candles from the top of the food dispenser, and he lit them with a lighter. He spaced them around the room.

"I'm told that these candles imitate the fragrances of heaven," Roger said. "Only one factory ever made them, and now that factory is broken down. It's a heap of rubble, in fact. The only way to get the candles is to search among the rubble."

"I've never smelled anything like it," Danielle

said. "It's somehow both sweet and crisp."

"Red 0.0, yellow 0.0, blue 0.0," Roger said.

The ceiling overhead went black, as did the ceiling over the street. The candles flickered softly and cast long shadows. Roger took two bowls from the top of the food dispenser.

"These were handmade by a master potter," Roger said. "No finer crockery can be found. Now, I recommend completely unseasoned food so that the candles' aromas dominate your senses. And I find that temperature 0.3 is optimal. The coolness desensitizes your tongue without being overly brash about it."

"I'll trust your recommendation," Danielle said.

"Sweet 0.0, salty 0.0, sour 0.0, bitter 0.0, temperature 0.3," Roger said.

He repeated the order and brought two bowls of food to the table.

"What temperature do you like your water?" Roger asked.

"0.7," Danielle answered.

Roger brought spoons and cups of water to the table. He sat across from Danielle.

"Well," he said, "try not to dislike it too intensely."

"Same to you," Danielle said politely.

She took a cautious bite. The candles' fragrance overpowered the slippery texture and bilious flavor of the food.

"This is almost tolerable," she said. "This is the

best meal I've ever had."

Roger smiled.

After they ate, Danielle rubbed her sore stomach.

"That really wasn't bad," she said. "If ordinary life can be this tolerable, then perilous adventures lose their appeal. I don't really want to leave this restful place of refuge. I'm unenthusiastic about returning to a world where warring factions agree about nothing but wanting to kill me."

"You don't have to leave," Roger said. "You could stay here. Rest as long as you like. You've earned it. You saved my life. I could fetch you books, paints, harmonicas, whatever you want. You can pursue leisure, as our forebears envisioned, in the comfort of a secure shelter with fine crockery."

"You know as well as I that our forebears envisioned no such thing," Danielle said. "And while it's tempting to give up now, grateful to have survived so many harrowing encounters, I really can't go back to a life of meaningless leisure."

"I was hoping you'd say that," Roger said. "Neither can I."

Neither of them spoke for a long time.

15

Cougar catches hold of Danielle's waist and steadies her thighs on his shoulders.

"Are you alright?" he asks.

"Yes," Danielle sighs. "I was just—just overcome thinking about the crypt nation. There are so many people, countless millions, suffering and trudging along below us, and they don't even know what they're missing. It just makes me ache."

"If you're not well, we can return another time for the remainder of the inscriptions," Cougar says.

"I'm okay," Danielle says, "and there's not much left. We came so far. It would be a pity not to finish."

"Then have some smoked deer to restore yourself," Cougar says.

He removes a tough, twisted strip from his pouch. Danielle chews it ravenously. Her flavored saliva dribbles from her lips.

"Remember your gratitude for the angel who gave its life to keep your belly full and your blood warm," Cougar chastens.

Danielle stops and coughs.

"Yes," she mumbles through her full mouth. "Of course."

"Here in the free nation," Cougar says, "we gratefully eat all foods: the flesh of the angels, the seeds and fruits of the archangels, and the flesh of the cherubs, the tiny, rooted cousins of the archangels. To the south, where the great fires flow, lies the cherub nation. The people of the cherub nation abstain from the flesh of angels. They maintain that angels are so similar to humans that to eat them is cannibalism. So they restrict themselves to the flesh of the cherubs and to the archangels' seeds and fruits. My little brother Panther spent some years in the cherub nation. To this day, he seldom eats angels. How we laugh at him! Even the angels eat other angels. Who are we to presume to be greater?"

Danielle listens and licks her fingers.

"To the north, where the rains are always cold, lies the angel nation. There, the people agree that angels are similar to humans. However, since the angels are more human, they must also be less divine than the majestic archangels and delicate cherubs. Therefore, it is less sinful to eat angels. So the people in the angel nation eat nothing but angels. I spent some months in the angel nation.

"Even further north, where the snows never melt, lies the ice nation. My elder brother Jaguar attempted to live there for several days. In the ice nation, there are steep mountains upon whose slopes the chilling winds forever howl. Upon the boulders of these mountainsides, naked prophets sit and stare all day at the great fire in the sky. They claim that we should aspire to be like the archangels, who draw all nourishment from the great fire and from the water in the land. These prophets abstain from all food and drink except for small mouthfuls of ice. Few indeed can live as they do! Many have died trying.

"At the base of their mountains are the camps of the aspirants. They may eat or drink whatever they like, but fires are forbidden. A preliminary attainment is the internal generation of warmth, so most of the aspirants wear as little as they can, and they sleep sunken in the snow. Before ascending the mountainside, an aspirant must lived naked in the snows for one week. If an aspirant disrobes but then puts on any covering, that aspirant must leave for a year before making another attempt. My brother Jaguar, though a fierce and mighty spirit, was able to remain naked for only three hours. Have you ever noticed that he has only nine toes?

"But as he packed his bundles to leave the ice nation, a prophet descended from the mountainside and worked many wonders. Wherever her bare feet stepped, the snows melted, and fragrant steam spiraled upward, coating her skin with moisture. She opened the eyes of the blind, healed broken legs, and counseled amazed listeners about how to quell hostilities in their homelands. Jaguar extended his frostbitten foot in supplication, but the prophet told him that the afflicted toe had a dangerous growth, and that he was now healed.

"I wonder, though, if Jaguar was hallucinating from the cold."

Danielle laughs.

"I'm about to hallucinate from the cold, if we don't finish here soon," she says. "Are you ready for the first fable? Okay. It's called The Raven and the Tower.

"In times long past, a raven stirred atop a tower. She pressed her wings upon the wind and spiraled from her roost. Above her there was sky, and below her there was sky, and anything on which the tower stood was too distant to be seen. She circled the tower, lower and lower, and its windowless walls were scraped and pitted from untold impacts. Whenever she tired, she returned to the top to perch upon the stone. And when the quaking of her feathers was only from the wind, and the heaviness in her claws was only from the stone, she set out again, always pressing a little lower, but no closer to the bottom.

"'Tower, who made you!' she called out during her descent. 'What secrets do you hold!' But the tower maintained its immutable silence. And the raven knew she had flown too low and hadn't the strength to return to the top. So she rested her wings and fell like rain. And the rush of the air forced shut her eyes, and its gusty embrace felt something like sleep. But before she dozed, did she smell the sea? And did she hear the roar of lions?

"And when she waked, she could no longer move. And when she tried, she could not even speak. And high atop her immutable silence, she heard a tiny rustling. It was a raven, stirring from its sleep. And the raven is mind. And the tower is matter."

"I used to think upon such things," Cougar says, "when I was six or seven years old and didn't know any better. How benighted were the people before the interment!"

"Cougar, be nice," Danielle says, her teeth beginning to chatter. "I still think upon such things. The next fable is called The Good Citizen of the Year.

"I heard about a ceremony to honor the Good Citizen of the Year. I decided to attend to see what it takes to win the award. I'd sure like to be the winner some day. A little public appreciation might help me overcome the bitter alienation that drives me to knock over trash cans in the park.

"The woman receiving the award had an impressive list of accomplishments: She once disguised herself as an antelope to lure an escaped lion back to the zoo, she plugged a hole in a gas pipe with her own head until help arrived, and she successfully performed the Heimlich maneuver on a toddler who had been choking on his own foot.

"I sat in the middle of the front row and listened attentively to her acceptance speech: 'I am grateful for the many opportunities I have had to help people. I used to try to find people to help, but the harder I tried, the less helpful I actually was. Now, I just relax. I no longer strive to be virtuous. I simply let events unfold, and I find myself being more helpful than ever. Why is life like this? I don't know. I just know that it is. My work comes to me, if only I trust it to.'

"After the audience applauded and began to disperse, I approached the woman. 'Is it really true?' I asked. 'Do opportunities to behave virtuously spontaneously come to you?'

"'I'm glad you approached me,' she answered. 'All evening, I've been wanting to tell you that your fly was down.'"

"That one has a lot of archaic terms," Cougar

says. "I'm not sure I understand it."

"That's too bad," Danielle says. "I could've understood it when I was just six or seven years old."

"Just read the next one," Cougar laughs.

"Okay," Danielle says. "This is called Effortlessness. When my sister and I were children, we once swam in the ocean. A powerful riptide carried us from the shore. Terrified, I swam against the current with all my might. I gradually expended the last of my energy, and I sank helplessly into the water. A few seahorses watched with passive indifference.

"My sister hauled me to the surface and kicked vigorously, keeping us both afloat.

"'How is it,' I sputtered, 'that you still have the strength to swim?'

"'While caught in the riptide, I surrendered to its superior power. I simply relaxed and let it carry me where it willed. Thus I conserved all my energy for when it was needed.'"

Danielle and Cougar remain in silence for a few moments. Danielle's breath comes in soft gasps.

"Okay, now I've regenerated enough energy to continue," she says. "The next one is called The Meaning of Life.

"In the heart of the desert lies an oasis where the Bahjghi people dwell. The Bahjghi live in almost complete isolation from the outside world, and their language is unlike any other on Earth.

However, the children are taught the language of the neighboring lands, and many of them choose to travel during their early adulthood. They never fail to return to their beloved oasis, bearing strange gifts and stranger tales of the outside world. Now, the Bahjghi language contains three words for 'ticklish,' but the word that means 'insurrectionist' also means 'argyle' and 'pancreas.' What's the moral of this story? That some things don't make any sense, and the search for meaning is a wasted pursuit."

"I used to believe such things," Cougar says.

"How old were you then?" Danielle asks. "Twelve or thirteen?"

"No," Cougar answers. "I was three."

Danielle laughs. "The next one is called Compassion. I read a book about the importance of compassion. I quickly made a sandwich and ran outside. I gave the sandwich to the first raggedy, unkempt man I saw.

"He threw the sandwich on the ground. 'I'm not poor, you idiot!' he shouted. 'I'm just raggedy and unkempt!'

"Mortified, I ran up to my apartment. I threw the book about compassion out the window. I heard a grunt and then a shout of gratitude. I looked out the window.

"'Thank you so much!' the raggedy, unkempt man said. 'Your book knocked out a mugger who was about to steal my Rolex! That's what happens when you throw compassion out the window: you effortlessly do the best possible thing!'"

"Ah, now that I still believe," Cougar says.

"Somehow that doesn't surprise me," Danielle says.

"I have a good reason for believing this," Cougar says. "I spent six months wandering unseen in the brigand nation. The brigands occasionally attempt to raid our camps, but they rarely do harm because their skills are so inferior to ours. Defense against the brigand nation is, in fact, the entire reason that there are warriors among my people. Wandering alone in the brigand nation is the final test in a warrior's training.

"While wandering, I discovered week-old tracks in the cold, dried mud and fallen leaves. Examining the tracks, I knew that they were made by a young woman who limped heavily. Fearing for her safety in this land of lawlessness and violence, I quickly followed the tracks. For one night and one day, I followed the tracks through a black swamp, up a wooded hillside, and down into a valley strewn with mossy boulders. Here, the tracks were very fresh, and I crept silently among the boulders. Hiding behind a dry, fallen trunk, I beheld the woman.

"I announced my presence, which led to a battle, for reasons I wish not to describe. As we battled, we conversed at length. Her name was Morel. She was from a band of women who are feared even among the brigands. Since there are no men in Morel's band, the women occasionally set out to harvest seed. I won't tell you how they accomplish this, but in the end, a man usually dies. Even I nearly fell to Morel's treachery. Luckily, my guard was up."

"Oh, is that what you call it?" Danielle says.

Cougar laughs.

"Let's get back to the doggerel," Danielle says. "My fingers are getting numb. The next bit is called Immortality.

"Seeking immortality is not bad unless you seek it outside yourself. If you seek immortality outside yourself, you will never find it within yourself. A part of all things is in you. A part of you is in all things. There is a part of you in the earth. There is a part of you in the moon. There is a part of you in the sun. The part of you in the earth transforms irreversibly. The part of you in the moon moves in endless cycles. The part of you in the sun shines forever in stillness. If you take the part of you in the sun into the moon, you move in endless cycles. If you take the part of you in the sun into the earth, you shine in stillness forever."

"I can honestly say that I have no idea what that means," Cougar says.

"Good," Danielle says. "Me neither. Do you think it's possible that the philodendrist knew something that you don't know?"

"I doubt it," Cougar says. "I am not even sure what to think about her. On the one hand, she led the pilgrimage underground, allowing the great congregations of archangels to resurrect themselves. On the other hand, I would not have willingly left this land. Nor would I have left unwillingly. I would have hidden and remained, as my ancestors did. If not for them, we would not be here now."

"The next part of the inscription alludes to this, however cryptically," Danielle says. "It's called The Longing of Our Spirit.

"We rely on machines to till our fields. We rely on machines to build our houses. We rely on machines to keep an exclusive record of our life savings. The more we rely on machines, the further we get from nature. The further we get from nature, the further we get from heaven and from the longing of our spirit.

"The wilderness is our anchor to the physical world. If all we needed was to enjoy our own ideas and our own inventiveness, we could be ghosts in the ethers, or robots in a manufactured world. The wilderness gives meaning to our bodies. The wilderness is the body of spirit.

"And so the wilderness is also our doorway to spirit, our doorway to eternity. But these doorways are closing as we destroy the natural places of the earth, and it's getting harder and harder to be whole, harder and harder to be well.

And it's terribly sad because it will take the earth many human generations to recover from our abuses.

"The road to hell is paved with pavement. Keep the ground God gave us."

Cougar nods. Danielle wobbles on his shoulders.

"Don't do that!" Danielle shouts. "You'll make me fall!"

"Sorry," he says. "I just didn't have any other response. Read the next part."

"Okay," Danielle says. "It's called The Complete Guide to Enlightenment. Oh! Well! That sounds useful. Here it goes.

"The only point of enlightenment is to be kind and compassionate—to people, to animals, to trees, to every living being. All the other commentary about enlightenment is just ornamentation. So if you want to know, for some reason, who's enlightened and to what extent, just observe people's behavior towards others.

"There is no need to wait for any further practice or any further training to experience what is known as enlightenment. It is the most natural thing in the world and the easiest thing in the world, as soon as all unnecessary striving drops away by itself. Let your true nature absorb you now.

"Effortlessness means seeing your life as a movie starring yourself. You enjoy the adventures, you enjoy the surprises, and you can even enjoy the danger because you know that a greater mind than yours wrote the script, and everything is going to be okay. Even as action is going on all around you and through you, you're as calm and relaxed as if you were comfortably seated in a theater.

"Gather every beginning experienced in your life. Gather every ending. Gather every full flourishing. Gather every hibernation. Gather all your merit. Gather everything you consider a mistake. And everything comes rushing into the center, and all the imbalances annihilate one another, and you're instantly reborn as your true self.

"Spirit wants everyone's life to be an epic adventure. However, spirit wants people to have the freedom to not believe in spirit. If people had obvious supernatural powers, we'd have no choice but to believe. Spirit makes our lives epic adventures in subtle, invisible ways, like coincidences and feelings.

"I don't know how to read the future, but the way to inhabit the best possible future is to be as present as possible in every moment, and to be as effortless as possible, to become an empty vessel through which your original spirit can flow. The spirit running through you is like gale-force winds. Just release all resistance, and let them move you. The gale-force winds will take you far.

Feel them now. Release whatever you're holding on to, to keep you from getting swept away.

"The human mind is good at certain things, like arithmetic, which can be useful. But somehow a mind with the power to do arithmetic is tempted to defy the superior power of spirit. Liberate yourself from logic and reason. There is a place beyond logic and reason. The whole universe is just such a place, and there your original spirit resides, and there your heart will find peace. As long as I sought answers outside myself, I was unsatisfied. Only when I recognized myself as an authority did I get the answers I needed.

"We all arise from mystery, and so returning to mystery feels like going home. Mystery doesn't have to be some far distant place or other dimension. Maybe the real mystery is the present moment, right here, right now, and returning to mystery just means entering the present moment fully, without any distracting thoughts about past or future.

"The hawk doesn't stop to eat the hare in midflight. Do one thing at a time."

Cougar says, "It is peculiar how people before the interment had to be told what is so clear and obvious. I wonder if they required detailed instructions about how to chew and swallow."

Danielle shrugs and rubs her cold hands over Cougar's scalp.

"I'm sorry," she says. "I'm just trying to warm my hands."

"That is fine," Cougar says. "I haven't polished my head for a while."

Danielle chuckles. "There are only two more sections to read," she says. "The next is called The Seeds of the Visions.

"We expect to endure so much grief and loss in our lives. We expect our pets to die. We expect our grandparents to die. We expect our parents to die. But the trees that we touch every week, every day—these we expect to outlive us. We expect our calloused, wrinkled fingertips to caress the same tree that shaded us in our childhood. We expect the trees to be the only friends from our infancy who will remain to comfort us as we die.

"And so when a tree is murdered, we suffer. But spirit did not give us our love for trees to make us suffer. The spirit that gave us this love will guide us all the way. The only way we can manifest the good that we crave is to release all burdens and accept effortlessness fully.

"If you make your life a waking dream of paradise, you help make the earth a waking dream of paradise. We must be the dark, fertile soil that guards the seeds of the visions we're given. Just by holding this space, we make it possible for the seeds to grow and the dreams to come true. As soon as you stop caring how things turn out, things turn out exactly as you'd want them to if you still cared.

"I do not offer solutions. I only offer prayers."

16

Danielle awoke, feeling refreshed, sitting in the chair in total darkness.

"Roger? Are you awake?" Danielle said.

"Yes," he said. "I've been awake for about an hour."

"Wow, you're quiet," Danielle said.

"It is incumbent upon the sentinel to practice stealth," he said.

"Maybe we should leave the light off while we think about our next step," Danielle said. "We might be able to concentrate better in the darkness."

"That suits me," Roger said. "I can start by telling

you what I've heard about the path of ascension. I probably know less than you because my goal was to obliterate information, not accumulate it. I've heard that the path begins in an exterior block, meaning a block on the exterior side of an exterior precinct. The obvious guess would be a block ending with J in a $z = 1.00$ precinct. But there are other possibilities, such as a block ending with A in a $z = -1.00$ precinct.

"I've also heard three riddles about the path: Look in only one eye. Ice, ice, why, why twice? And, three different letters, three different numbers."

"I've heard those as well," Danielle said, "though not all from the same source. Had you also heard that the three coordinates of the path were hidden in three different blocks?"

"Yes, though I wasn't sure which the three blocks were," Roger said. "Different path seekers searched different blocks. Maybe some of them were deliberately trying to throw me off. I don't know."

"Well, my source was good," Danielle said. "Based on what I found, I'm pretty sure I searched the right blocks. If my inferences are good, the z coordinate is 1.00, which is what we'd expect for a path to heaven, and the y coordinate is 0.43. For reasons I don't want to mention, I don't have the x coordinate."

"Three different letters, three different numbers," Roger recited. "The three letters must be x, y, and z! This riddle is telling us that the three coordinates are three different numbers."

"What good does that do us?" Danielle asked. "There are still 199 possible values of the x coordinate."

"Okay. That's right," Roger said. "Let's think. We have all the information we need, I'm sure of it! We just have to piece it together. There's something we're not seeing in the two remaining riddles."

"Ice, ice, why, why twice?" Danielle said.

"Look in only one eye," Roger said.

"That's it!" Danielle exclaimed. "I can't believe it! You solved it!"

"I did?" Roger said.

"Yes! Look in only 1I! This is actually specifying the block! We're not given the first letter of the block, but the middle number is 1, and the last letter is I!"

"But blocks that end in I are below blocks that end in J," Roger said. "So even though the precinct's z coordinate is 1.00, the block we need is not a top block in the precinct."

"So the block we need must be an exterior block in the x or y direction!" Danielle said.

"And it can't be the y direction because y = 0.43," Roger said. "This precinct is adjacent to other precincts in both the plus y and minus y directions."

"So the block we need must be exterior in the

x direction," Danielle said, "so the unknown x coordinate must be either -1.00 or 1.00."

"And it can't be 1.00 because that's the z coordinate," Roger said.

"So it has to be -1.00, so the block we need must be on the minus x side of the precinct," Danielle said.

"So the block must begin with A, so the path must begin in the A1I block of the x = -1.00, y = 0.43, z = 1.00 precinct!" Roger shouted in the dark.

They sat silently. Danielle rubbed her damp palms against her thighs.

"We know exactly where to go," she said. "I wonder if we're the first. Who am I to contemplate ascension? I'm just a normal girl with chronic diarrhea. I'm unexceptional in every way."

"I'll prepare," Roger said. "Red = 0.0, yellow = 0.0, blue = 0.2."

Dim blue light gleamed from the ceiling. Roger dialed the combinations to the padlocks on the chests. Danielle reflexively memorized the numbers. Roger slung two guns over his shoulders. He buckled a satchel of ammunition around his waist. He reached into the second chest and placed two transmitters in his pockets.

"Roger, I'm scared," Danielle said.

"Don't worry," Roger said. "When the sentinel and the high heretic unite, their success is assured. The chariot of heaven awaits, though only one will ride upon it."

"Is that a prophecy from antiquity?" Danielle asked.

"No," Roger said. "I just made that up."

Danielle giggled. "It's funny, I so wanted to believe the first part of it. I thought it was a real prophecy."

"It's easy to make people believe what they want to believe," Roger said. "It may be useful to remember that. In the absence of wisdom, people cling to foolishness."

He looked around and adjusted his straps.

"Well, are you ready?" he asked.

Danielle stood. She took Roger's hand in her own.

"I'm afraid that this won't end well," Danielle said. "I'm afraid that your prophecy may be more accurate than you thought. I just want to say that I'm grateful I saved your life. I forgive you for trying to kill me. I'm honored to have you beside me. I don't want to have to finish this without you."

"Don't worry," Roger said. "I'll be with you to the end."

But he looked away, and his cheeks were wet. He cleared his throat.

"Taxi!" he called.

17

Roger instructed Danielle as they rode through the tunnels. "As we walk, I'll watch the space ahead of us, and you watch the space behind us. Keep an eye on windows, doorways, alleys, intersections, anywhere someone could suddenly appear. Pay attention to all vehicles and drones. If people are around, watch their hands. Could they have any guns, knives, or transmitters in their pockets? If you see anything suspicious, tap my shoulder. The harder the tap, the more immediate the danger. As you pull your hand from my shoulder, try to sweep it in the direction of whatever you noticed. Try not to let the adversary know you're on to him. If necessary, whisper in my ear.

"I'll be ready to draw my guns. You be ready with the transmitter. You're pretty skilled with it. Take this one. It's higher in the hierarchy than most. For as long as possible, we'll make sure we're within sight of a vehicle with a known identification number. We'll make the taxi follow us if we don't see any vehicles. Do you have any questions?"

"What about a medic vehicle?" Danielle asked. "Shouldn't we make a medic follow us in case of emergency?"

"I hadn't thought of that," Roger said. "That's a good idea. Let's call for one as soon as we get out of the tunnel. Use the transmitter to keep it near us."

They rumbled onward in the darkness. Danielle tugged absently at her safety belt. She fiddled with her hair. Finally, she grabbed Roger's hand. They sat in silence for some time.

"I can't stop thinking that I'm the wrong person for this adventure," Danielle said. "I'm so lacking in useful abilities. I'm not a champion athlete, so I can't outrun, outmaneuver, or outpunch anyone. I'm not a scholar, so I can't draw upon a vast reserve of information. I feel destined to fail where others may have succeeded. I feel like an unexceptional girl confronted with an exceptionally perilous challenge."

"The only people who feel exceptional are

exceptionally arrogant," Roger said. "Just do your best. That is what has gotten you this far. And see how far you've come! Doing your best will continue to buoy you, all the way to the end."

After some time, the taxi slowed, and a tunnel door opened ahead of them. Danielle immediately gagged at the stench.

"Medic!" she choked. "I might really need one!"

The odor intensified when the taxi door shut behind them.

"This is a good sign," Roger said. "The path should be hidden somewhere people are unlikely to wander by accident. If someone visited this block as a random exploration, the visit would surely be brief. Let's get out of the taxi. We'll have a better view around us."

Windowless buildings lined the street. The rumble and squeak of machinery was audible through the walls. No vehicles or pedestrians were on the road.

"Roger! The tunnel door is opening!" Danielle said.

"Position the taxi between us and the tunnel door!" Roger said.

He drew both his guns and pointed them at the tunnel. Danielle used the transmitter to position the taxi as a barricade. A medic vehicle rolled out from the tunnel. Roger lowered his guns, and Danielle halted the medic.

"Okay, let's cautiously investigate the block.

Make both vehicles follow us. Or should I control one of them?"

"I can handle it," Danielle said. "I'll use a separate transmitter for each so that I don't have to keep retyping identification numbers."

Roger strode down the street with his guns drawn. Danielle followed, holding a transmitter in each hand. The taxi kept pace at their left flank, and the medic traveled at their right. They passed several side streets. To Danielle's horrified astonishment, the smell continued to worsen. Behind them and to the left, the door to a building began to rise. Danielle forcefully tapped Roger's left shoulder and dragged her hand back. Roger wheeled and aimed his guns at the opening door. Danielle positioned the vehicles defensively.

A cart rolled out of the door. The cart appeared to be loaded to the top with excrement. The door lowered behind the cart, which then turned down a side street. Danielle and Roger looked at each other. They smirked and shrugged. They turned to follow the cart.

"I always wondered what happened after we flushed the toilet," Danielle said.

They trotted after the cart. It passed a dozen windowless buildings and veered toward a building on the left. The door rose immediately before the cart passed through, and the door lowered immediately afterward. Danielle and Roger paused to catch their breath. The taxi and medic idled patiently.

"I'm sure we're on the right track," Roger said. "It makes perfect sense that the path would be hidden where an unwitting explorer would never go. No one would catch a ride in one of those carts unless there was a really good reason for it."

"I'm actually considering it, which proves just how determined I am," Danielle said.

"I don't think there's any other way in," Roger said. "The two sides of the building are blank, and the back seems to be up against the wall surrounding the block. The door is unmarked. We could try the ten thousand possible identification numbers for the door, but we don't know what happens when we try the wrong ones. Possibly nothing happens; possibly the door explodes. If I were designing this door, I would make it lock downward in response to a false identification. If this happens, then we'll never get in."

Another loaded cart approached. Roger reflexively aimed his guns at it and then relaxed.

"Well?" Roger said. "Do you want to hop in?"

"Wait! Watch this!" Danielle said.

She tapped rapidly on the transmitter buttons. The taxi and medic moved to block the cart's path. The cart attempted to circumvent them, but they repositioned themselves to thwart it.

"If only we had some kind of giant scoop, we could empty out the cart before we got in," Danielle said.

"How about bashing the cart from side to

side with our vehicles?" Roger said. "It might tilt enough to spill most of its contents."

"Great idea!" Danielle said.

The taxi and medic bashed the cart from side to side. Thick waves of filth splattered in all directions. Danielle doubled over and retched, but she continued to control the vehicles.

"I think that's as good as we'll get it!" Roger said. "We'll only sink to our knees."

Danielle positioned the vehicles to pin the cart in place. With her gloved hand, she held the edge of the cart and jumped inside. She slid in the muck and nearly fell. Still holding both guns, Roger took a running leap into the cart and landed with an unfortunate splash.

"I appreciate the derring-do," Danielle said, "but I think my face would be a lot cleaner right now if you had simply lowered yourself in."

Roger laughed with a touch of hysteria. "We're so close," he said. "Don't be concerned with aesthetics."

Danielle and Roger crouched in readiness to duck under the doorway, and Danielle directed the taxi and medic to move out of the way. The cart sloshed forward, the door rose, and they entered the building. The door slammed shut behind them.

18

The cart traveled down a hallway to a T intersection and turned to the left. Danielle and Roger jumped out of the cart. They both slipped on the filth coating their shoes, and they fell into each other. Roger quickly righted himself and pointed his guns in opposite directions.

"Now that we're in the building," he said, "I'd guess that we don't want to go where the cart goes. It's probably headed to a legitimate sewage facility."

They crept down the hall. Roger aimed both guns forward, and Danielle frequently glanced behind. They heard hissing and crackling sounds, and they came to a room. Water rippled in a pool beside the far wall. Crackling blocks of ice floated on the water, and dense mist rose from it. A vehicle stood in front of the pool. Unlike familiar vehicles, this one had a completely sealed interior. A thick, curved window sheltered the seat.

"How do we get inside that thing?" Roger said.

"I don't know," Danielle said, "but at least we can wash off."

She walked to the pool and extended her hands into the mist. She gasped and retracted her hands.

"It stings!" she said. "The mist is so cold that it stings!"

"I guess swimming is out of the question," Roger said, walking to stand beside her. "The vehicle is probably here to take us through the water."

"An unmarked vehicle," Danielle said. "Listen—did you just hear something?"

"It's just the ice creaking," Roger said. "Try to relax. We need to concentrate. We need to figure out the vehicle's identification number."

"Ice, ice, why, why twice?" Danielle said.

"That's right," Roger said. "That's the riddle we haven't yet used."

"And the ice is right here," Danielle said. "So now's the time to use this riddle. But what does it mean? What happens twice?"

"This is the first ice pool we've seen," Roger said. "Do you think we missed one somewhere?

Should we go down the other hallway?"

"Listen—I heard it again!" Danielle said.

Roger spun around, pointing his guns back at the hallway. Then he relaxed and turned to Danielle.

"Leave the vigilance to me, and try to stay focused on the riddle," Roger said. "You solved the last one. I'm counting on you to shine once again. I never would have figured out the pun in 'one eye.'"

"That's it!" Danielle said. "You got it!"

"Actually, I didn't," Roger said. "But I can see that you did."

"It's another pun!" Danielle said. "Ice, ice: y. y twice! It's the y coordinate! We have to use it twice! We're in $y = 0.43$, and the only way to use it twice in a four-digit identification number is to make 4343!"

"I'm a little concerned about dropping the zero and the decimal point, but I think you must be right!" Roger said. He grinned broadly.

"I can see that you're as inept at vigilance as you are at portraiture," said a man arriving from the hallway.

He was bald, and his cheeks were hollow. He wore a fuzzy blue bathrobe and matching slippers. He was flanked by six men pointing guns at Roger.

"Whose petulant whimpers are these?" Roger sneered. "Oh, the baby's, of course. I thought I smelled a dirty diaper."

"I weary of our banter," the warden said.

The warden raised his hand and pointed at Roger. Roger tried to raise his guns, but he was too slow. He fell with six bullet wounds in his abdomen. He screamed harshly and ceased suddenly.

"What obnoxious screams!" the warden said, rubbing his ears. "Ear-splitting! Blood-curdling! Simply dreadful. I always knew he was an ill-mannered fellow."

Danielle's bones rattled with fear, but she drew upon her final reserves of valor.

"As a courtesy to my murderers, I pledge to keep my dying screams as soft as possible," she said.

"I shall soon appreciate that," the warden said. "Before you perish, I suppose I should thank you for solving the final riddle. I've known of this vehicle for some time but did not know how to unlock it. I'd thought to circumvent the vehicle, so I threw several people in the icy water, but their bodysuits froze solid, and, immobilized, they drowned. Anyway, your usefulness to me has ended, and so has my sponsorship of your endeavor. You surely didn't think you achieved so much on your own.

"Now, how long shall I let you struggle before I make you die?"

"The last person who said that to me suffered an unenviable fate," Danielle said through clenched teeth.

"I weary of our banter," the warden said. "Let's see if you uphold your pledge to scream softly."

He raised his hand.

"After I use the secret rhythm to type the identification number," Danielle said.

The warden paused.

"I know of no secret rhythm," he said.

"That's the point," Danielle said. "That's why you can't kill me yet. This unmarked vehicle requires the secret number to be typed in a secret rhythm. One small misstep, and it self-destructs."

"Very well," the warden sighed. "Tell me the secret rhythm."

"That would take decades!" Danielle said. "I've been trained from birth! You cannot imagine the precision with which I must type the four simple numbers. I've felt the rhythm in handshakes, I've seen the rhythm in winks, I've heard the rhythm in fife solos. Surely you don't think you're the only one who knew I was destined to arrive here. A plan set in motion generations ago is finally spiraling to its inevitable completion. And though you will kill me as soon as I activate the vehicle, I will witness the fruition of the glory of my lineage."

"Yes, yes, very glorious," the warden said. "Now get on with it."

Danielle pointed a transmitter at the vehicle. Her hand trembled with fear that she did not have to feign.

"Kindly instruct your gunmen to lower their

guns," Danielle said. "I can't type the right rhythm when I'm shaking with fear."

The warden grunted irritably but nodded at the gunmen. They lowered their arms.

Danielle breathed deeply, ignoring the stench. She watched her fingers until they stopped shaking. Then, as fast as she could, she typed 87654321. The first four numbers triggered a loud pop and a puff of smoke from the vehicle. The last four numbers constituted the emergency shut-off command. The ceiling light went black.

"Kill her!" the warden screamed in the darkness. "She destroyed the vehicle on purpose!"

"But Wardy," one of the gunmen said, "we can't see anything. We might shoot you by mistake."

"That would seem to be a legitimate point," the warden said. "Someone give me a gun!"

Danielle tore off her clothes and dived into the icy pool. She nearly fainted from the shocking cold. The frigid water stung every inch of her skin and forced her eyes to shut. Her hair froze solid and tugged painfully at the roots. Aching numbness gripped her fingers and toes before she even began to swim downward. She felt the wall for any opening. Icy knives of pain scraped her throat, and she choked down a scream. The cold invaded her ears and crushed her skull, as though her brain were packed in ice. The cold penetrated deeper inside her body. Her kidneys and stomach contracted painfully. Sharp pangs tore her bladder.

She had trouble knowing if her legs continued to kick. She had to exert all her will each time she dragged an arm through the water. She descended deeper. Suddenly she noticed that she had been still for several moments, lost in a kind of daze. She forced herself onward.

Her lungs ached for breath, and she involuntarily sipped some water into her mouth. The cold burned her tongue and sent stabbing pains into her teeth. She wept through clenched eyes and prepared to surrender to death.

She felt an opening in the wall. She hauled herself through it. She kicked off the bottom of the opening and swam upward with hollow arms. The cold penetrated her heart. She felt every heartbeat like a hammer smashing a block of ice. Her arms and legs were so numb that she detected her motion only as a subtle churning sound in her ears.

Her head burst the surface. She hoarsely gulped air, scraping her throat with the violence of her inhalations. Her eyes would not open. She flailed about for the edge of the water. She discovered it by bashing her head against the wall of the pool. Now she could open her eyes. She flung an arm up onto the floor. Her fingers were twisted into a strange contortion, and she could not feel them. Her other arm flopped up onto the floor. She kicked desperately to raise herself out of the water, but she began to slip back down.

Screaming as loud as she could, she hoisted herself onto the floor.

As soon as she cleared the water, a door lowered behind her, isolating her from the icy mist. She shivered, curled on the floor. Her teeth chattered loudly. Ahead, she saw a vehicle, similar to the one on the other side of the pool. This one, however, was illuminating the area with a bright light, and its top hatch was opened. It faced away from the pool.

Danielle crawled toward it. Her legs were too numb to support her. On a whim, Danielle said, "Temperature 1.0." Heat poured from the inside of the vehicle. As numbness melted from her skin, prickly pains lashed her, but she reveled in the return of sensation.

She climbed into the vehicle. A transmitter lay on the seat, but the vehicle had already responded to a vocal command. She sat, and a safety belt slithered around her hips.

"Close," she said.

The hatch closed.

"Temperature 0.7," Danielle said. Temperature 1.0 had already begun to feel excessive.

She rubbed her hands over the plush seat. She rubbed her feet and her face. All sensation had returned. Everything left behind felt like a long, chilling nightmare. She smiled.

"Take me to heaven," she said.

19

She slept. She had troubling dreams of guns and knives, caustic fumes and gagging odors, flat walls and right angles, a pervasive sense of lifelessness, an unshakable feeling of wrongness. She knew, however, that she was about to awaken.

When she opened her eyes, the vehicle was still. A pool of water was just ahead.

"Open," she said, and the hatch opened. The safety belt retracted from her hips.

She tested the water with her foot. It was cool but not cold. She stepped into the pool. The water rose only to her thighs. The touch of the water enlivened her. She felt that she was being cleansed. She walked through the water. She came to a wall, but below the surface of the water, she found an opening to a submerged tunnel. She took a deep breath and swam.

After about a minute, the tunnel opened into a larger pool. Danielle stood up and breathed deeply. Tears streamed from her eyes. She had never smelled air like this before. There was no hint of exhaust or staleness. She smelled a sweetness and a crispness. The air blew across her wet face. She began to cough, great heaving coughs that rattled her ribs. She spat out stinking phlegm. The coughs ceased at once. She breathed, feeling a new softness in her lungs and belly.

She moved through the water. Beneath her feet, the ground was alternately soft and pebbly. The varying sensations in her feet enlivened her further. She looked up. The ceiling was very dark, but not uniformly. To one side, there were many small pinpoints of light. The other side was grey, ending in a pinkish orange.

Danielle stooped to rinse her face, and some of the water dripped onto her tongue. She gasped at the pleasure of the flavor. She took a cautious sip, and then she gulped wildly. She had never tasted water like this. There was no oily residue, no bitterness, no affront to her tongue or throat. She drank until her belly swelled.

She paused. No longer splashing, she heard a flurry of sounds in all directions. A whizzing became a kind of whirring, and then a hooting came from another direction, and just when a sort of fluttering was subsiding, a spate of cackling burst forth. The ceiling seemed to brighten, and she saw silhouettes moving through the air, supported by nothing at all.

"The angels," she murmured, awestruck.

She waded onward. The water became shallower. Several paces ahead, she saw splashes that she did not create. She paused, but she could not determine the source of the splashing. She continued walking. As her feet made contact with dry ground, and water dripped from her hair, she saw her first archangels.

She dropped to her knees in wonder. She had never seen anything so large. They towered above her far more than she towered above an infant. The archangels swayed and stretched languorously, rustling in a majestic symphony. The archangels' gigantic fingers strummed shafts of brilliant light.

Danielle rose reverently and approached the archangels. The closer she came, the smaller she felt. Small pebbles pressed into her feet and held her attention to the ground. She came upon the archangels' long toes, meandering and burrowing beneath the surface. Diffident, she brought her toe into contact with an archangel's.

Joy and exhilaration swept through her. Arms extended, she ran until she touched the nearest archangel with her hands. The archangel was so wide that she could not see around it. She looked upward, and she could not see its top. She leaned against the archangel.

She could feel its breath, deep and slow, seeping far beneath her feet. She could feel its antiquity, the innumerable days it had seen. She could feel its kinship with the other archangels in its congregation. She could feel their mutual adoration and admiration. She felt its lineage, extending back into timeless mystery. She felt its bond with its progeny, some already ancient themselves, some yet to be born, some populating a vast, unseen future. She felt its near indestructibility, its brushes with peril, fires, floods, rushing air. And in a small pocket in the distant past, she felt its grief over the slaughter of its forebears.

"I'm so sorry for what we did to you," Danielle said. "So sorry, so sorry. It will never happen again."

She held herself close to the archangel, and though its lowest arms were far above her, she sank into its embrace. She began to feel some hunger. She did not know where to find food in heaven, but somewhere in her blood, her ancestral memories held the answer. It was her birthright to survive here. She would learn whatever was necessary.

The ceiling continued to brighten, and she

caught her first glimpse of the great fire above. She stared in amazement, and when she looked away, a green echo of the fire danced in her eyes. The ceiling seemed to be round, not flat, and there were no flat walls or right angles.

She began to run through the congregation of archangels. The choirs of angels sang loudly all around her. Some scurried away as she ran, and some were indifferent to her. She gulped the pure air hungrily, greedily. She ran faster, pumping the purity of her surroundings into her body. The ground was unlevel and occasionally abrasive, but the sensations in her feet spurred her to greater exertion. The congregation of archangels seemed to extend forever. Each one was more majestic than the last. Danielle laughed out loud as she ran.

The ground collapsed beneath her feet, and she fell into a pit. She yelped at the pain in her heels. The walls of the pit were smooth and about ten feet high. An archangel's thick toe, six inches wide, spanned the top of the pit. Danielle leapt and brushed the toe with her fingertips, but she was unable to grip it. The floor beneath her was crumbly, and she tried to form a mound to stand on. However, the mound was too soft, and it flattened beneath her feet.

Danielle lay on her back and caught her breath. She enjoyed her view of the ceiling. It was a great, radiant blue, so bright that it hurt her eyes if she stared too long. Strange white puffs hovered and drifted across the ceiling. Danielle smiled exuberantly. A prison in heaven was better than a palace in hell.

The hairs on the back of her neck prickled. She was being watched. She stood and peered upward but saw only archangels.

"Who are you?" she called.

"We are people of the free nation," a man's voice responded. "We had not expected one of the crypt-born to possess such keen powers of perception. We can see that you are exceptional for your kind."

"Actually, I'm unexceptional in every way," Danielle said. "Would you mind explaining why I'm in a pit?"

"We have failed to reach consensus as to what to do with you," the man answered. "Some believe that we should welcome you as an equal. Others contend that we should slay you before you endanger our community. Still others, seeking compromise, counsel us to hold you in captivity until the necessary course of action becomes clear."

"If I wanted petty bickering among stubborn factions, I would have stayed where I was," Danielle said. "You should be ashamed of yourselves. Here among the archangels, you should have hearts of pure love and magnanimity."

After a pause, the man spoke. "We admire

fearlessness, and we recognize the probity of your remonstration. We have decided to accept you as an equal.

"We know that there are many barbaric customs in the crypt nation, and we would like to instruct you in our way of life. Here, take this."

A tunic tumbled into the pit.

"We are accustomed to covering much of our bodies with something we call clothing," the man said. "Clothing serves many purposes for us. It keeps us warm. It keeps us dry. It shields us from the great fire above us. It protects us from sharp or abrasive surfaces. It can contain pouches in which we carry useful tools. Soon you will come to appreciate the many uses of clothing. If you can't figure out how to put it on, we will send down one of our women to help you."

Danielle took one end of the tunic and slung the other end over the archangel's toe above her. She gripped both ends and tugged hard, hoisting herself out of the pit. She stood and clad herself in the tunic.

"I think you'll find," she said, "that I'll be quick to adapt to your ways."

She reveled in the sound of amazed murmurs. Faces emerged from shadows, and strong arms extended, welcoming her home. In the hearts of the archangels, a light shines forth, a beacon to all who would rest.

20

Danielle sits upon Cougar's shoulders. The sky becomes purplish gray, and twisted yellow clouds scurry across the west.

"This is it," Danielle says. "The last of the inscriptions. I suppose that this is the last writing I'll ever see, now that I'm out of the crypt nation."

Cougar leans his head into Danielle's left thigh.

"We have an ancient proverb," he says. "'What goes up must come down.' These inscriptions are not all that is written in stone."

"What are you saying?" Danielle says, panic creeping into her voice. "That I must return to the crypt nation? I hate that place! You can't imagine what I went through to get out. I never want to go back!"

"We have another ancient myth," Cougar says. "From time to time, and for the benefit of many, the divine must sacrifice itself and descend into sorrow."

"Oh," Danielle says. "Then I'm safe. I'm clearly not divine. I just passed gas on the back of your neck."

Cougar laughs, but then his voice rasps in his throat. "I, too, am less divine than you might imagine."

Danielle wonders at his sadness.

"But maybe," Danielle says, "for the sake of adventure, we can together infiltrate the crypt nation, and pretend that many will benefit."

Cougar does not answer, and a cold wind blows in Danielle's heart.

"I need to get down from this mountain," Danielle says. "Here is the final inscription, The Prayer of the Philodendrist.

"Merciful Creator, I thank You for trees.

"I thank You for the snow-laden forests, the rain-drenched jungles, the wooded hillsides, the black-watered mangroves, the sand-swept palms, the island thickets overlooking pebbly coves.

"I thank You for the towering elders whose skyward branches conspire with storm clouds and consort with starlight.

"I thank You for the forest floor blanketed with acorns, elders waiting to arise.

"I thank You for the preserves, the refuges, the sanctuaries, the parks.

"I know that one day You will resurrect the great forests of the Earth: forests that stretch thousands of miles in all directions. Forests threaded with streams, lakes, rivers, boulders, valleys, glades. Forests that all will revere as the temples You built for Yourself.

"I hope I live to see this day.

"But if a sapling could leap out of each of my hairs, and if an ancient tree could spring from each drop of my blood, and if each of my sinews could split into acres of forest, and if a million trees could crack out of each of my bones, then sow me like seeds in the soil of the Earth."

Acknowledgments

I received beneficial guidance from Amy Benson Brown and Elizabeth Galu of the Author Development Program at Emory University.

Jason Breyan came up with the chilling directive, "Take the feet first so the rest can't run away."

My mom edited the first draft.

John Malko and Laura Griffin proofread a later draft.

A number of phrases and concepts were borrowed from Tracker School (trackerschool.com), Healing Tao (healingdao.com, bostonhealingtao.com, taohealing.com, healingqi.com, universaltao.com), Laozi, and Zhuangzi.

About the Author

Jed Brody is a Senior Lecturer in Physics. His short fiction has appeared in *Creative Loafing* and an anthology of *Science Fiction by Scientists*. His essays have appeared in *Physics Today, the Philadelphia Inquirer*, and *One Hand Does Not Catch a Buffalo: 50 Years of Amazing Peace Corps Stories: Volume One: Africa*.

He was a Peace Corps volunteer in Benin, West Africa, where he taught high school physics and chemistry. He studied solar electricity at Georgia Tech. As a member of a US-Tibet Science Initiative, he traveled to India five times to teach physics to Tibetan monks and nuns.

He enjoys yoga, qigong, birdwatching, swimming, and reading, but usually not all at the same time.

Are you a changemaker?

Stories about our world, and our relationship with nature, have been communicated among wise souls and changemakers for countless generations.

People willing to courageously make a difference in the world have gathered around campfires and sat under the limbs of mighty trees to be nurtured by this wisdom. Story is how humanity has always shared moral tales, empowered itself with knowledge, and paid hope forward into the future.

Our authors embody this spirit. They write with reverence, wisdom, and inspiration about the places, plants and animals, habitats and ecosystems, of our shared home—*Earth*.

In our new online place—*The Gathering*—you can connect directly with our brave authors and other bold thinkers to unshackle creative action. We all hold the power to make positive change. We just need a safe space to soar like feathers in the wind.

To connect with brave authors, like Jed Brody, join *The Gathering* now.

www.stormbirdpress.com

Stormbird Press is a proud signatory to the **United Nations SDG Publishers Compact**. At the time of publishing this title, our focus in on contributions to *SDG 13: Climate Action, SDG 14: Life Below Water, SDG 15: Life on Land,* and *SDG 16: Peace, Justice and Strong Institutions.*